# Augie Sweetwater and the Dolphin's Tale

## WILLIAM J HARRIGAN

ISBN: 978-1-942739-14-2 paperback

ISBN: 978-1-942739-15-9 ebook

Cover design by Damonza.com

Editing services by BubbleCow.com

# Chapter One

CALL ME COOP; all my friends do. Mostly on account of my real name, which is Yardley Holdsworth Cooperlick. Not much in that pond if you're fishing for a nickname, right? So call me Coop and let me tell you about my new friend Augie Sweetwater.

He was the first kid I met on Monday morning, the last day in August. It was day numero uno at the Anacortes School for me because my family moved up here from Seattle over the summer. If you're not familiar with this part of the world, we're what you call the Pacific Northwest. Check the map and you'll find us in the upper left corner of the US, looking out over Canada and Puget Sound. The San Juan Islands are right on our doorstep. The water around here is beautifully clear, but oh man is it ever cold. Be prepared if you jump in for a swim – your goose bumps are gonna have goose bumps.

So anyway, just a few minutes after we met, Augie and I were killing some time on the wooden bench outside the principal's office. Right off the bat I discovered that Augie is even worse off than me, name wise. He told me his full name is Augenblick Sebastian Sweetwater. Can you imagine the grief he's taken over that? A shy, short, skinny eleven-year-old with glasses and a naughty monogram?

So I asked him about the Augenblick thing 'cause I'm kind of interested in weird names, which you can understand from my own. Augie said it came from a German poem called *Augenblick*. A love poem he said, his mother's favorite. He recited the last line of the poem for me and it went like this: *Dann habe ich dich gefunden und alles hat sich im augenblick verändert.* Course, I just looked kinda blank until he translated it, which as it turns out went like this: *Then I found you and everything changed in the blink of an eye.* See, augenblick is German for blink of an eye.

I guess I should mention, by way of explaining why Augie and I were waiting on the principal, that the second kid I met at the Anacortes School was George Banner. He had grabbed poor Augie by the front of his shirt, lifted him about a foot off the floor and slammed him against the hallway lockers. Now this Banner is a big guy, with a big gut straining a heavy leather belt on his blue jeans. He had his nose into Augie's face and was spitting out a string of stupid threats. As I came up behind him, I heard the last one, and although it was hard to understand because Banner was growling like an angry bear, it sounded like, "Or else I'm gonna break your twiggy neck and toss your egghead in the trash."

I stepped alongside Banner and tapped on his shoulder. He snapped his head in my direction, still holding Augie against the wall. He had one big mitt on Augie's neck and was pushing so hard that Augie's eyes were bulging, and his face was turning blue. Banner snarled that I should mind my own business, so I did. I broke his nose.

Banner wasn't sitting on the bench with Augie and me, seeing as how he was further down the hall at the nurse's office where they were taping an aluminum splint to his face, which I think will make a good addition to his stupid mug. Man, I hate bullies.

So the principal – whose name by the way is Candice Treneger and I'll bet nobody ever called her Candi in her life 'cause she's got jet black hair, eyes as dark as a hungry tiger and looks like she eats kids like me for breakfast – called me in. She sat me on one of three banged-up metal folding chairs that had been lined up in front of her desk. It was so uncomfortable I wondered if she'd bought the set surplus when they closed the prison at Alcatraz. She settled in behind her desk and we looked each other over for a minute or so.

I decided I had been wrong about the tiger thing. She looked more like a raven. A big, black-feathered bird with a yellow beak and an attitude. Maybe it was because her hair was cut close to her head and it was kinda flying away on the sides, which looked to me like feathers lifting in the wind. Plus, her thin fingers and sharp nails looked like talons. If you squinted a bit.

When she inspected me, I'm guessing she saw a four-teen-year-old boy with some size to him. I'm pushing six feet now and starting to fill out in the shoulders and chest. Sandy hair, neatly cut. No ponytails or buzz cuts for this kid. No way. Blue eyes that work just fine, so I'm lucky enough not to need glasses. Green plaid shirt, old jeans and well-worn Adidas trail-running shoes. It's not like there's a lot of money for clothes in our house, but it wouldn't matter if there was. I'll take comfort over style any day.

When Mrs. Treneger finished her inspection of me, she cocked her head like a crow might. Then she blinked twice, also like a crow might, if crows blink. First thing she did was dispense with the nose busting event, waving it away with a little flutter of her fingers that didn't even amount to a light slap on the wrist. Then she started telling me about Augie. Seems like besides being named after German poetry, Augie's smart. Not just ordinary smart, but über-smart if we're sticking to Deutsch.

Mrs. Treneger said, "Mr. Sweetwater is off the scale on every intelligence test. He's going to make more discoveries and invent more wonderful things than Leonardo Da Vinci, Albert Einstein, Thomas Edison and George Foreman combined, provided he doesn't trip over his own shoelaces and fall down the stairs, or accidentally step in front of a speeding car."

She stopped there to see if I was taking all this in.

I nodded and said, "Call me Coop."

Then I spun my finger around to let her know she could pick the pace up. She pursed her lips into a shape that to my imagination was distinctly beak-like, then she leaned forward and shifted up a gear.

"Now here's the thing, Mr. Coop. Augie's mother is dead, and his father is in prison."

I gotta admit, she caught my full attention, dangling skeletons from Augie's closet like that. I sat up a bit straighter on the Alcatraz torture chair and waited for her to put some meat on the bones of this story.

She said, "Augie's mother was an heiress, Mr. Coop.

Her name was Rose, and she was the only child of Simon Silver, whose grandfather founded Silver Shipping way back in 1932. The ships are gone now, but Rose was worth more than three hundred million when she . . . well, when her husband strangled her."

I could feel my eyes go big and round.

"No sh . . . kidding?" I said.

"No shidding," she said with the tiniest of smiles.

I was starting to like this old bird. Which was good, since I was probably going to be in her office a lot.

"Really?" I said. "Augie's father killed his mother?"

"And three other women," she said. "Strangled them all. Don't you remember? It was on all the news channels for months."

"No, ma'am," I said. "My mom says the news will just make you sad or crazy or both, so we don't watch much of it. And I don't know much about what's been happening in Anacortes. See, we just moved here from Seattle. To be with dad number four and a half."

"Of course," she said. "I should have realized when I saw your name on the report slip. You are our new ninth grader. It will take you some time to get to know Anacortes."

She leaned even further forward and fixed me with those raven eyes. Maybe it was just my imagination again, but I swear she tilted her head like a bird to look at me with one eye first and then the other.

"But . . . dad four and a half?"

I nodded.

"Kevin Coleman. He owns a charter boat for fishing, diving and whale-watching." I pointed over my shoulder in the general direction of the biggest marina in Anacortes. "A forty-foot flybridge cruiser called *Golly Gee*. He keeps it over in the Cap Sante Marina, on the commercial dock. He won't be dad five officially until after the wedding." I could see skepticism radiating from her face, so I added helpfully, "In October."

She let the almost smile creep in again and leaned back.

"How's that working out for you?" she asked.

"Dandy," I said, meaning it. "Kevin's also a dive instructor and because of him I have my scuba diving certification. All my dads are cool like that. And since mom and I are still in tight with all of them, it's like having five fathers."

"Four and a half," she said.

My turn to almost smile.

"Four and a half," I agreed.

She glanced down at some papers on her desk, which I took to be the report of this morning's incident and probably my student info. I hoped I wasn't getting off on the wrong foot at my new school, but man – I think I said this before – I hate bullies.

Mrs. T said, "I see you enjoy climbing, Mr. Coop. Isn't that rather dangerous, especially for someone your age?"

"No, ma'am," I said. "I mean yes, I enjoy climbing, but no, it isn't dangerous."

"You never fall?" she said, cocking her head and raising an eyebrow. I made a mental note to check later – do crows have eyebrows?

"All the time, Mrs. T," I said. "But I don't climb on cliffs or boulders. I'm into speed climbing."

She fixed me with her eye and raised the eyebrow

another quarter inch. I figured I'd better get to the point quick or she'd run out of eyebrow-raising room.

"Speed climbing is an inside sport, on a climbing wall. With a safety harness and cushy mats. When you slip off the wall, which happens like I say, all the time, the person holding the safety rope lets you down to the mat, light as a feather."

"Ah," Mrs. T said.

Just to be helpful, I added, "It's an Olympic sport now. I'm too young for this go round, but come next Olympics I'll be over sixteen and I want to be there."

Mrs. T regarded me thoughtfully for another minute or so, then she nodded like she'd come to a decision. She put the report papers away and folded her hands on her desk.

She said, "Since you have more than the normal allotment of fathers, perhaps you can share with Mr. Sweetwater."

"Absolutely," I said. "But, uh . . . if his mom's dead and his dad's in jail, where is he living?"

"Mr. Sweetwater lives in his late mother's home, of course. In the daily care of one of Rose Sweetwater's most loyal retainers. Legally, he is currently the ward of Benjamin Kensington, his deceased mother's attorney," she said.

I gave that a quick mulling over and said, "Well, that's good, isn't it? He must be the guy in charge of the money too."

"Very good, Mr. Coop. He does indeed hold the keys to the Silver Shipping fortune and he's honest as the day is long and scrupulous to a fault. The problem is that he's ninety-three and lives alone in a house in Washington Park on the far side of town. Although he's quite sharp mentally, he's practically a recluse. I fear that Mr. Sweetwater, like you, should be counting his fathers in fractions, only going down, not up. You might say he's on half a dad and fading."

"No sweat, Mrs. T," I said. All in all, I thought it was a pretty cool situation. There have been times lately when I would have enjoyed that kind of space. "I like that kid," I said. "I'll keep an eye on him for you. What grade is he in?"

"Ninth, Mr. Coop," she said. "Same as you."

"Ninth grade?" I said, "But Augie told me he was eleven years old. And the reason I asked him about his age, ma'am, is 'cause he looks like he's maybe nine, tops."

She pushed her chin out at me, turned her head to the side and gave me the crow eye again.

"Tell me, Mr. Coop, what else did you observe about Mr. Sweetwater?"

I rubbed my forehead, cause it helps me think sometimes. I've found that it also gives me some extra time in which to do that thinking. So I rubbed and ran my memory loop back about an hour and tried to picture Augie as I first met him.

"Let's see," I said. "Short and skinny. Sandy hair sticking out everywhere, like maybe he'd lost his comb a couple weeks ago."

I stopped rubbing and ran a hand over my own head, just in case I had a bunch of stray strands poking out where they shouldn't, but I didn't, so I went on with my description.

"Big cocker spaniel brown eyes behind thick glasses with plastic tortoise shell frames." I smiled at Mrs. T and said, "I half expected to see that he'd repaired them with a Band-Aid and a safety pin, but nope." She didn't smile back, so I hurried on. "No pocket protector either, but he was wearing an un-tucked red T-shirt that looked a size-and-a-half too big and brown corduroy pants with the legs turned up at the bottom. Blue socks and shiny black shoes."

"Very good, Mr. Coop! That's our Augie all right," she said. "Now listen. Augie is only here for one reason. Before she died, his mother insisted that he attend junior high and high school among his peers. She wanted him to have a normal upbringing." Mrs. T raised her chin and rolled her eyes. "That hasn't been exactly possible. If Augie has any peers, you won't find them here. You see Mr. Coop, although Augie has never actually finished high school, he has a doctorate in nano-engineering from the Massachusetts Institute of Technology. By the time he finally gets his high school diploma here at the Anacortes School, he'll also have earned a second doctorate in biomedical engineering. He accomplished most of the work for those prestigious degrees online, starting when he was seven years old. He also worked on his degrees at MIT during the three summers that he spent in Boston under the care of the only other member of the Kensington law firm, Benjamin's younger brother, Harold."

She gave me that piercing raven look again, perhaps to reinforce the seriousness of the matter.

"I say younger brother, Mr. Coop," she said, "but you should understand that I mean relatively speaking. Harold is ninety-one. Time is running out on Augie's living arrangements. He's the smartest kid on planet Earth, but he doesn't know how to look after himself. He's going to need your help."

# Chapter Two

MRS. T SENTENCED me to an hour of detention every day for the next week for punching George Banner because "You must realize Mr. Coop, that we cannot tolerate fisticuffs at Anacortes School," but the sweet old bird counted the time served in her office and put me on probation for the rest. Provided, of course, that I weld myself to Augie. I thought that wouldn't be any great hardship, especially later in the day, when Augie invited me to his house for dinner. Mom was making tuna casserole, which I would take any excuse to avoid.

Did I mention that we were picked up after school by a chauffeur in a sleek, black polished-to-perfection Mercedes? The driver, a fit-looking old gent in a gray suit with gray hair and an impeccably trimmed gray moustache, introduced himself as Mr. Bartholomew. I got the impression that before he took the gig as Augie's chauffeur, he'd been driving for Augie's mother. And he'd probably been doing that since the first Ford Model T hit the streets. Mr. Bartholomew opened the cavernous trunk of the Mercedes and my mountain bike fit inside with no problem, after I took the front wheel off. He carried us away from school in that whisper-quiet cocoon of a car, which let me call my mother with my cell phone and fill her in on developments.

Her response?

"Of course, Coop. Visit your new friend. Be home by eight to do your homework before bed. We'll save some casserole for you in case you're still hungry."

Super, I thought. When I ended the call and put the phone back in my pocket, Augie said, "If you don't mind, we're going to make a stop on the way home."

I shrugged. Here I was being chauffeured around in luxury, why should I care?

"No sweat," I said. "Where to?"

"My friend Michael has a match this afternoon. I promised I'd be there."

"A match? You mean like a boxing match?"

For some reason that tickled Augie. He sat back in the leather seat and laughed.

"No, definitely not boxing – fencing."

"Fencing?" I said. I had a picture in my head of two cowboys stringing barbed wire from post to post in Wyoming, their hobbled horses munching prairie grass while they waited, a big blue sky in the background. How that sort of endeavor qualified as a competition I didn't know.

"Not making fences," Augie said as though he had seen the cowboys in my head. "Sword fighting."

"Oh yeah, swords," I said. "Excellent!"

The venue for the match was on the other side of town, on the highway out toward Deception Pass. It was a long, low building with double glass doors in front and a neat line of spruce trees down each side. One door had the letters USFA written on it in large, bright red letters. Underneath were the words *United States Fencing Association*. A sign taped to the other door announced that today's matches were for the *Regional Youth Circuit*.

Mr. Bartholomew let us out in front. I looked back just before the door closed and noticed that he had waited until we were inside before motoring off to park. I had to hustle after Augie. He had apparently been here before, because he hurried through the lobby and headed straight to a set of small bleacher style seats in the main arena.

"Just in time," he whispered as we parked ourselves near the bottom of the bleacher, in the only empty seats left. Two fencers were ready to begin, standing on either side of a referee. At his signal, the crowd quieted, and an aura of anticipation settled over the place. I have to admit, I'd never seen a fencing match before, and it was fascinating.

The two fencers faced each other on a long, narrow mat directly in front of us. Both were wearing white canvas uniforms, with a mesh helmet that protected their heads and concealed their faces. The fronts of their torsos were covered with a finely woven gray mesh. They both wore heavy gloves on their sword hand. I noticed that one of the fencers was left-handed.

Both fencers also had a cord attached to their back, which connected them to a scoreboard on the opposite side of the mat. Augie quietly explained that when you touched your opponent's torso with the tip of your sword – it's called a foil, actually – you scored a point. A match lasts eleven minutes, three periods of three minutes each with one-minute rest in between, or until one person scores fifteen touches.

The action was lightning quick. So quick in fact that I missed most of it until my eyes adjusted to the pace and I learned what to watch, which was the hands and the tip of the foil, not the body of the fencer.

Michael, who Augie pointed out as the left-handed fencer, was good. Actually better than good, at least to my untrained eye. He was always on the attack, always seeking out any target his opponent left open. And I've never seen someone so light on his feet. He seemed to glide above the mat, like one of those superfast magnetic trains. After the first two periods, he was ahead eleven to three. Halfway through the last period he scored his fifteenth touch and the match was over.

Augie jumped to his feet and applauded wildly, so I stood with him and clapped too. Michael bowed to his opponent and slipped off his mesh helmet. When he turned to face us, I was hit by a thunderbolt.

Michael was a girl.

Not just a girl. Michael, at least to my inexperienced adolescent eye, was a stunningly beautiful girl. When she had taken the helmet off, her long black hair had fallen free, cascading over her shoulders in a soft wave. She had large, luminescent brown eyes, high cheek bones and a smile that could melt all the ice in Antarctica if global warming doesn't do it first. She unhooked her wire and floated over to us, still moving with that magnetic smoothness she'd shown in her match. Augie stepped down from the bleacher to meet her and they gave each other a big hug. I went to join them, tripped on the bottom step and nearly fell on my face.

Michael covered her mouth with her hand to stifle a

giggle. Augie didn't seem to notice my clumsiness. He held a hand out from Michael to me and said, "Michael, this is Coop. He saved me from that obnoxious Banner fellow this morning." Augie looked at me and nodded toward Michael. "Coop, this is my friend Michael Anne Deerwood. She's a Lummi princess."

"A Lummi princess?" I said.

Michael Anne gave a lilting, musical laugh and shook her head.

"Don't mind Augie," she said. "He tells everyone that." She touched a finger to her fencer's uniform and said, "I'm a Lummi Indian, yes. But Augie made up the princess bit."

"Her father is a chief and the head of the Lummi Cultural Commission," Augie said to me. "I think that makes her a princess." He turned to Michael Anne and smiled. "A princess and a champion," he said. "Congratulations on your win."

"Thanks," Michael Anne said flashing a brilliant white smile. "I'm not a champion yet, but now I get to compete in the statewide youth match in Edmonds next week."

"Then you have time for a game tomorrow?" Augie said.

"Double chess? Absolutely."

Michael bumped fists with Augie. Then she nodded at me and said, "Nice to meet you, Coop."

"Nice to meet you too, Michael," I said.

She smiled, then chuckled, which was not as musical as her laugh but still very nice. Like someone softly humming a short melody.

"Augie calls me Michael for fun." She reached out a lightning quick hand and lightly punched Augie on the shoulder. "My mother calls me Michael Anne to get my attention." She stretched the same hand out to me and said, "My friends call me Mika."

"Coop," I managed to croak. I was so tongue twisted by her beauty I probably sounded like I was choking. I was half afraid she'd feel compelled to start the Heimlich maneuver on me.

"I didn't see you in any of my classes today," I said, trying to sound normal. "Do you go to Anacortes School too?"

"Oh yes," she said, "but I'm in the eighth grade, one behind you and Augie."

"Ah," I said, sounding absurdly lame even to myself. "Have you known Augie long?"

"Forever," she said with another lovely smile. She leaned over to kiss Augie lightly on the cheek, then she said, "When Augie's mother was alive, my mother was her personal assistant. She brought me to work with her quite often, especially on weekends. I'm only two years older than Augie, so we usually played together."

My muddled mind managed to do the math and I was delighted to discover that Mika was thirteen, only a year younger than me. She said goodbye to both of us, then turned and danced away. I could swear the temperature dropped three degrees when she was gone.

"Double chess?" I said to Augie as I watched Mika float through the door to the locker rooms. "What's that?"

"I wanted to spice the game up," he said, "so I built a chessboard that is twice the size of a regular board. Then I doubled up all the pieces on each side. Except for the king and queen, of course. There must be only one king and one queen for each player, or you would have chaos."

"Of course," I said, thinking that chaos was going to be a frequent state of mind if I hung around with Augie a lot. We left the hall as the next pair of fencers were being introduced and stepped outside. The Mercedes purred up right on cue, as though Mr. Bartholomew had been expecting us exactly at that instant.

# Chapter Three

"HOME?" MR. BARTHOLOMEW asked when Augie and I were belted into our seats in the back.

Augie, who was already tapping away at an oversized iPad that he had plucked from a pouch in the seatback in front of him, looked up and said, "Yes, please." Then he pushed his glasses up on his nose and went back to whatever he was doing on the iPad. I leaned over casually, you know so as not to seem nosy, and took a peek. Augie was zooming, moving, cutting and pasting faster than I could follow on a drawing that seemed to have dozens of different colored lines. If I had to guess, I'd say it was either a wiring diagram or a really wild tattoo. My money was on the wiring diagram.

I sat back and enjoyed the ride as Mr. Bartholomew drove us back through Anacortes, past the Cap Sante Marina where my new dad-to-be docked his boat, the *Golly Gee*. Mr. Bartholomew continued driving, out onto a stretch of land on Fidalgo Bay that was empty except for two or three large brick buildings. A walking path wound its way along the waterfront down this way and I'd already discovered that it was a great place for a jog. In addition to the view, there was a series of Washington State Park educational signs along the path that I could use as an excuse to take a break. One of them had old photos of the logging industry that had flourished here in the early 1900s, until the Great Depression of 1929 killed it deader than dead. This area had once been prime real estate, but now it was mostly empty weed-covered lots, except for the old buildings I mentioned.

Mr. Bartholomew turned into a narrow driveway between two of those waterfront buildings. The one to the left was clearly one of the logging era buildings; a long, stout structure of weathered red brick with high ceilings. The aluminum-framed windows suggested a recent remodeling, as did the elaborate wrought iron bars that protected them. The front door was a massive affair that looked like it had been constructed using every inch of wood from a very large oak tree.

The building to the right was evidently Augie's house. It was set back a bit more from the road, allowing for a porch and a tiny yard with a couple of rhododendron bushes sporting thick bunches of green leaves. In contrast to its mostly brick neighbor, this building had been constructed entirely out of stone. The designer had included some arches and intersecting roof lines that gave it a bit of a Victorian mansion vibe, but there was no disguising its utilitarian original purpose. Especially when there was a large, hand-carved and brightly painted sign hanging from the porch that read: *Anacortes Fire Department, Established 1890.* Below that another line announced: *Anacortes Morgue, Established 1891.* A bronze plaque on the corner of the building certified that it was on the national historic register. How cool is that, I thought. I'd heard of people living in converted barns and churches before, but never a renovated building that had been a combination fire house and morgue.

Mr. Bartholomew opened the back door of the car on the side closest to the fire department's front entrance – or maybe it was the morgue's, but I didn't really want to think about that – so that Augie and I could both climb out. While I was lifting my bike out of the trunk, two men burst out from behind the rhododendron bushes. While I watched in amazement, one grabbed Augie and threw him over his shoulder, the other lunged for Mr. Bartholomew.

Then two things happened, both fast and unexpected.

First, Mr. Bartholomew reached into the jacket of his tailored gray suit and pulled out something that looked like a ray gun from one of the latest outer space movies. He pointed it at the assailant who was about to tackle him, and a streak of blue light shot out from the gun, accompanied by a loud *Zzaappp*! Mr. Bartholomew hit the man dead center in the chest with the blue light. The guy instantly went loose and hit the driveway like an eighty-pound sack of the potting soil my mom uses in her garden.

Second, I snapped out of my daze and swung the frame of my mountain bike at the legs of the guy who was trying to carry Augie away. I caught him right behind the knees as he was running past me and he let go of Augie. Mr. Bartholomew's guy had gone down in silence, except for the thud his forehead made on the driveway, but mine hit the ground with a lot of cursing. Mr. Bartholomew shut him up with another shot from his blue zapper thing.

We stood Augie up, gave him back his glasses and dusted him off. After he got the glasses adjusted on his nose, Augie seemed to be fine. He hitched his pants up and grinned at me, like this sort of thing happened every day. For all I knew, maybe it did.

Mr. Bartholomew gave me an up and down inspection then said, "Well done, Mr. . . . ah?"

"Coop," I said. "My friends call me Coop."

Mr. Bartholomew stuck out his hand and said, "*My* friends call me Bart. Pleased to make your acquaintance, Mr. Coop."

The way he said *Mr. Coop*, with a delicate combination of respect and poking fun, made me wonder if he was related in some way to Principal Treneger, who had pronounced it exactly the same way in her office at school. As I watched Bart retrieve Augie's backpack from the rear seat, I realized he might be getting on in years, but he still moved like an athlete. Just a bit more measured in his motions. He straightened up with the pack in one hand and held the other out toward the door.

"Shall we go inside?" he said.

Augie nodded casually and headed up the porch steps. Bart followed him. I looked around; a bit mystified as you might you understand.

"Uh, what about them?" I said, pointing at the bodies of the two attackers.

Over his shoulder Bart said, "Oh don't worry. The police will come and remove them."

"They're not dead then?" I said, hurrying to catch up.

"Dead? Oh no. Of course not."

He slipped the little gun from his jacket again and showed it to me.

"Augie invented this little gem. Shoots a bolt of energy that stops a person's muscle control. Interferes with the spinal cord somehow. Augie can give you all the science involved, but if you understand a word of what he says you're a better man than I. Anyway, I call it the Blue Blaster."

He handed the little gun to me. I was amazed at how light it was. And how it seemed alive in my hand. If it was plastic, it was some kind of plastic I'd never seen before. You might think I'm crazy to say this, but the Blue Blaster seemed to tingle and squirm against my palm. It reminded me of my Aunt Lucy's Jack Russell terrier – you know, always jumping out of its own skin.

Bart took it back and held it up so that he could admire it himself. "Effective range is only twenty feet, but it produces instant, total relaxation. Heart keeps beating, of course and they can breathe normally. Also, the . . . ah . . . butt muscle stays on the job. So there's no mess back there."

"Fortunate," I said.

"To be sure," Bart said with a small smile and a quick upward flick of his eyebrows.

He put the Blue Blaster away and turned to follow Augie through the front door.

"However, they do always seem to wet their pants," he said. Then he shrugged. "The muscular effect wears off completely in about an hour, about the same time the trousers are dry."

"Say Bart," I said. "What if those attackers had guns? Don't you worry about Augie getting shot?"

"Why would they shoot Augie, Mr. Coop? They are kidnappers. They need him alive."

"Kidnappers?" I said. "How do you know that?"

Bart sighed, and I got the distinct feeling that this was an old story.

"Augie's father sent them," he said. "He arranges for this to happen all the time, even though he's in prison." Bart sighed again. "He wants to control Augie's life. And Augie's money."

"So he sends kidnappers," I said, finally getting the picture. "But those two out in the driveway didn't seem like the smartest pair on the planet. What if they took a shot at you and hit Augie by mistake?"

"Good point," he said, "and that is precisely why Augie always wears bullet proof shirts."

I'm pretty sure I stood there with my mouth hanging open, perhaps even drooling a bit. I finally snapped it shut and said, "Bullet proof shirts?"

Bart smiled, then turned his head toward the stairs, where Augie had gone to change clothes.

"Augie," he called out, "perhaps you would like to demonstrate your shirt to Mr. Coop?"

Augie came bouncing back down the stairs, dressed in a dark blue t-shirt, a different pair of corduroy pants rolled up at the cuff like before and black canvas sneakers. He stopped next to me and ogled me through his thick glasses. Then he picked up the bottom of his t-shirt and held it out to me.

"Feel this," he said.

I took the material and rubbed it between my fingers.

"Feels like cotton," I said, "but stretchy." I shrugged my shoulders. "Not much different than any other t-shirt."

Augie shook his head.

"That stretchiness you feel is actually millions of nano-robots woven into the shirt."

"Robots?" I said. I must have looked ridiculous, with my eyebrows up in the middle of my forehead and my jaw down around my navel.

Augie just laughed, a warm laugh that I would eventually discover was his way of expressing delight when one of his inventions amazed his friends.

"You're thinking of a metal human-like creature, perhaps one like 3-CPO from *Star Wars*." He shook his head. "These robots are microscopic. They are made mostly out of carbon and silicone. Very simple robots, because they have only one job: to pull themselves together. See, most of the time, they relax. So the garment feels comfortable, even slightly stretchy as you so accurately noted. But . . . when a bullet touches the shirt, they instantly pull together. They bunch up in less than one hundredth of a microsecond."

Augie snapped his fingers, although even *I* know snapping your fingers takes way longer than a hundredth of a microsecond.

"You would feel a firm poke from the bullet, but that's all. The shirt will grab it, absorb all its energy, then toss the bullet back with a gentle lob."

Augie illustrated the whole thing by making a sudden fist, shaking it and then extending his fingers, like he was rolling dice.

"Best to wear the shirt loose rather than tucked into your trousers, so that it is free to move and bunch up. If you do that it will work on almost any pistol, up to a .44 magnum," he said. He shook his head once and added, "Not so good for rifle bullets."

"But Augie," I said. "A .44 magnum? Isn't that the gun from the *Dirty Harry* movie? The one Clint Eastwood's character says is the most powerful handgun in the world?"

I did my best Dirty Harry imitation when I said that last part, but I guessed that Augie has ever seen the movie, because he didn't get it.

Augie shrugged and said, "I doubt that the .44 magnum is the most powerful handgun in the world, but yes, it's plenty powerful. In fact, a Remington .44 magnum bullet weighing 180 grams leaves the barrel of a six-inch revolver with 1,036 foot-pounds of energy."

"Oh," I said. I didn't know what those numbers meant exactly, but I figured it must be a big punch. I was amazed that what felt like a simple cloth t-shirt could stop that kind of power. Also, I was really amazed that anyone, much less a kid who won't be able to vote for seven years, carried that kind of information around in his head.

Augie ran his eyes up and down my torso, then reached up and put his hand on my shoulder to turn me around. He said, "I'm thinking you'd be a size large?"

I nodded, still flabbergasted by the entire episode. At least by this time I'd gotten my jaw closed and my eyebrows settled back where they belonged.

Augie looked up at Bart and said, "Would you mind getting a half dozen shirts for Coop from the storeroom?"

Bart nodded – actually he bowed slightly, just like you see butlers do in the old movies – and said, "Of course. Six shirts, size large, assorted colors."

He saw my bewildered look and spared me having to ask another stupid question.

"Augie made the prototype here, of course, but the shirts are made at his manufacturing plant in Detroit. We keep a supply on hand." Bart tilted his head toward the building next door and said, "Augie, I know you want to show Mr. Coop around your lab. You two go ahead. I'll make sure the police clear the clutter off the front yard, then I'll fetch the shirts for Mr. Coop and begin preparing dinner."

Augie was already on the move to the building next door. "Grab your bike," he said over his shoulder. "You can leave it in my lab for now."

I could hear a new excitement in his voice, so I hurried after him, scooping up my bike on the way. Augie casually stepped around the would-be kidnappers, still motionless in the yard, and I followed him.

# Chapter Four

**As we walked,** Augie explained that his family's company, Silver Shipping, had owned all the land on this part of Fidalgo Bay for many years. Once there had been warehouses, docks and railway lines, but it had all been torn down, except for the buildings that were now his home and his laboratory. I'd seen that his house was protected as an historic landmark and now standing next to the lab, I could see why it also hadn't been torn down. Two stories high, two blocks long and a full block deep, it was constructed of bricks laid over a foundation of large, close-fitting granite blocks. With numerals a foot high, the date 1903 had been etched into the cornerstone block of granite. Well over a century old, I thought, and this place would still win any wrestling match with a wrecking ball.

The door to Augie's lab was also impressive. The ancient oak wood had hardened over time into a granite-like solidness to match the rest of the building, but whoever made the door had not been content to let it go at that. Thick steel straps had been added every six inches across the door and around the entire perimeter. I noticed the door was set into a frame made of the same heavy steel. I didn't think you could breach that door with a tank.

Rather than open the door itself, Augie turned to the wall on the right. He stuck both hands into flaps that were set into the stone.

Looking over his shoulder at me he said, "This is one of my inventions. It's an improvement on the type of lock that reads hand imprints. Sensors inside check all ten fingers and both palms for the correct prints. But this lock also checks my pulse and compares it to the electrocardiogram that's on file."

A green light illuminated over the door and the lock released with a solid thunk as Augie withdrew his hands.

"What would happen," I asked as he pushed the door open, "if somebody besides you stuck their hands in that thing?"

"Oh," Augie said, "that's another improvement. If the lock doesn't recognize me, it grabs the intruder by the wrists and notifies the police. They are trapped here until the police arrive."

I gave the twin flaps a quick glance as I followed Augie into the lab and made a mental note to myself: DO NOT stick your hands in those grabby-things unless Augie programs them for you.

We walked into the lab and the big door automatically closed behind us and locked itself with a loud thunk. The lights must have been programmed with the door, because the whole lab lit up in sequence: click, click, click. Augie's lab was the most amazing place I'd ever seen in my life. I leaned my bike against the wall and trailed in after him.

The lab looked partly like a NASA control room for a

mission to Mars with a dazzling array of consoles and flat screen monitors, and partly like an automated assembly line for expensive cars with multi-armed robotic machines. The whole place hummed with a muted concert of cooling fans, spinning computer drives and quiet pumps. There were two levels, but much of the lab was open in the middle. An elevator large enough for a bus climbed up one corner and a sturdy metal railing ran around the open part of the second floor to keep people from falling off. On the first floor, I recognized a couple of stations that used computer aided design and computer aided manufacturing because Dad Two used similar stuff to build his custom cars. You could draw something on the computer, and then the computer would use a laser or water jet to carve it very precisely out of a block of metal or plastic. Slick. Augie had six of them, ranging from one about the size of a cell phone to one about as big as a king-sized bed.

I also recognized a drill press and a band saw, but that was about it. The rest of the gear in the lab was beyond me. One feature that I found particularly fascinating was a water channel that entered the lab from Fidalgo Bay. It was located on the far side of the lab and was enclosed behind a long glass wall, probably to keep the salt air away from all the sensitive equipment in the lab. I could see that the water was high in the channel, which I assumed was because the tide in the bay was high. I knew the tide rose and fell an average of about five feet at the nearby Cap Sante marina, so I estimated that the water channel in the lab would be cut off from the bay at low tide. The channel inside the lab looked quite deep though. Even when the entrance to the bay was cut off by the tide, I thought the water that remained in the cut would be at least ten or twelve feet deep. Before I could ask what the channel was for, Augie hooked my arm and guided me to an open room with comfortable leather chairs and a large table. It seemed to be a combination lobby and conference room, a place to either take a break or have a meeting. One wall was lined with display shelves.

"These are some of my latest inventions," he said. I caught a strange pitch in his voice and when I looked at him, I could see he looked stiff and tense. I slapped myself on the forehead – mentally anyway – when I realized that of course he was tense. This poor guy never got to strut his stuff for his friends.

I slapped him on the back and said, "Dang Augie, this stuff is so cool."

I pointed to a thing that looked like a deflated football with a purple Mohawk.

"What the heck is that one?"

"That's something I invented for my friend Ray. He came down with acute myeloid leukemia when he was five. He's in remission now, but he had to go through a lot of chemotherapy and lost all his hair."

"Man, that's tough," I said. "Does he go to our school?"

"Oh, no," Augie said. "He lives in Phoenix, Arizona. He's one of my online friends."

Augie picked up the Mohawk thingy and held it out. I could see now that it was actually a flesh colored headpiece, not a football. Augie turned it inside out and showed me that the underside was lined with thousands of tiny, tiny knobs.

Holding it over his head, as though he was about to put

it on like a hat, Augie said, "When you wear this device, it stimulates hair growth. Normally, it would take a healthy person a few weeks to grow a small nubble of hair, longer if you've just finished a heavy course of chemo. Wearing this, Ray grew two inches of hair in less than twenty-four hours."

Augie carefully replaced the device on the shelf.

"Of course," he said, "hair is made of a protein called keratin, and no one grows hair out of nothing. So I made up some special protein shakes and sent them out to Ray. He said they tasted like . . . well, never mind. The hair grower worked just fine and now I provide them to cancer clinics all over the world."

"Why the purple Mohawk?"

Augie laughed. "Oh, that was Ray's idea. I was going to put regular hair on it, but Ray said no way. I discovered later that he was right. The atmosphere in a cancer ward can be stifling. In a hospital, sometimes you need a dose of outrageousness to get through the day."

The next piece of gear looked like an ordinary travel bag except that it was orange. Not just orange, but a vivid orange that made the purple Mohawk look tame. It had a hard-shell case, wheels and a retractable handle, like the kind of luggage you can carry-on and stow in the overhead compartment on an airplane. At Augie's invitation, I pulled the handle up and rolled it back and forth. I didn't think it was very heavy; thirty or forty pounds maybe.

"Pretty fancy luggage," I said. "Guess it will be easy to spot among all the black bags on the luggage carousel."

"Well it is easy to spot," Augie said. "But I had to get a special waiver from the Transportation Security Administration in order for people to carry it onto aircraft cabins."

"Really? How come?"

"Here let me show you," Augie said.

He took the bag from me and laid it on the floor. Then he flipped up a couple of latches on the side and opened it. The entire lid was hinged on the side, so it opened like a clamshell. The inside was . . . well, you weren't going to get your socks and underwear in there. The top two thirds were taken up by a device that was densely wrapped with tubing of some kind. The bottom third had a control panel and four electrical sockets. They looked like standard sockets to me, the kind you'd use for a lamp or a power saw. Between the control panel and the sockets there was a metal gadget that looked vaguely familiar. It was round and about three inches across.

"This is an electromagnetic generator," Augie said. He pointed at the gizmo on the top, the one with all the tubes wrapped around it. "The outside part of this assembly is the magnetic engine. It's powered by propane and has only one moving part, a spindle that is suspended on magnets inside the engine. Since the engine is basically round, I was able to design a compact generator that fit inside it. The controls and electrical hookups are on the bottom, as you can see."

"What's this little dealy-bob?" I said, putting my finger on the round thing.

"That's a standard propane diaphragm," Augie said. "You use it to attach a regular twenty-pound tank of propane."

"Oh, like the kind my dads use on the grill."

"Exactly," Augie said. "It's a worldwide standard fitting for propane tanks, so you can use this generator anywhere."

"How long will it run on a single tank?" I asked.

"That depends on the electrical load of course. The more things you run with it, the more fuel you use."

"So . . . on average?"

"Well, the maximum output is twenty kilowatts. But let's say you're only running a refrigerator, a television and two light fixtures with LED bulbs." Augie was quiet for a moment and I could almost see the gears turning in his brain. "One twenty-pound tank would last for five days, nine hours and twenty minutes. Approximately."

"Five days! That's amazing, Augie."

The lighting in the lab was so bright that it was easy to see Augie blush.

"You must be making a ton of money with inventions like these," I said.

"Oh, no," Augie said. "The components of that generator are very expensive and assembling them is difficult. We do that in Detroit, where Mr. Kensington helped me set up a factory." He paused to give a little shake of the head. "Fortunately, or perhaps I should say unfortunately, there is plenty of commercial space available in Detroit and the city has many skilled people who want jobs. Anyway, it costs us $3,257 to make each one."

I whistled.

"Wow, that is a lot. Well, they are phenomenal little units, real life savers. But I guess you don't sell very many for that kind of dough."

Augie shook his head again and added a little chuckle.

"Actually, we sell them as fast as we can make them to the Red Cross for three hundred dollars."

"Three? Did you say three hundred dollars Augie?"

"Yep. You see Coop, I invented those after Hurricane

Maria hit Puerto Rico in 2017. I have another computer friend named Mateo who lives in a little town called Arecibo on the north coast of the island. The hurricane came across Puerto Rico from the south and flattened his entire town as it left to the north. Mateo's mother had suffered a stroke a few months before the hurricane hit and she needed a ventilator to breathe."

Augie stopped to take a deep breath, but I could guess where this story was headed.

"They had tried to be prepared, but they only had a small generator with two days' worth of gasoline. They couldn't get even one more gallon of gas until four months later. Four months, Coop. Mateo helped bury his mother four days after the hurricane."

"You practically give these miracle generators away . . . just so that won't happen again?"

"Well . . . yes."

I thought about the hair grower and wondered what the numbers were on that. Augie saw where I was looking and preempted my question.

"The hair grower is also made at our Detroit factory. It costs $747 to make. Unfortunately, it's disposable. Each unit only works once. We sell them to cancer clinics for $74."

"Holy . . . cow, Augie. Aren't you going to go bankrupt?"

"Oh gosh no, Coop. My corporation is making plenty of profit from other items, like the bullet proof shirts."

"I see," I said, suddenly discerning another layer of this wonder kid. Imagine this if you will: a skinny eleven year old who re-invents chess because it's soooo boring, dresses like he's colorblind and impoverished, is bullied by dipsh . . .

dipshids who are after his lunchtime baloney sandwich and is the CEO of a thriving technology company. The bullies call him a nerd; man I'm gonna be delighted to call him my friend. I've got remember to thank my mom for moving us to Anacortes.

"What's this?" I asked, moving along the displays and pointing at a large square-ish steel box with an open front that glowed blue along all four sides. Beyond the glowing opening I could see that the bottom was a polished steel tray about two feet by two feet.

"That's my recycle bin."

"Seriously? How do you get it out to the curb on re-cy-cle day?"

Instead of answering directly, Augie pushed a button on the top right corner of the thing. A panel along the top slid back, revealing a winking set of LED lights in blue, green and red. A power readout showed the device was plugged into 220 volts. Another small panel illuminated one word: READY.

Augie walked over to a workbench further down the lab and returned with a hunk of metal about the size of my shoe. Holding it out to me he said, "This is solid aluminum. 7075 aluminum to be exact. It is one of the highest strength aluminum alloys and we frequently use it in aircraft."

I took the block carefully, thinking I'd never expected to hear an eleven-year-old say the words "we frequently use it in aircraft." When I hefted it, the block certainly seemed light. But solid, too.

Augie took it back from me and stood in front of his recycle device. He made sure I was watching, then lobbed the block straight in.

I jumped straight up.

When the aluminum block passed through the blue opening, there had been a loud crack and that's what made me jump. I moved over next to Augie so that I could look into the opening. The recycler unit seemed to have gotten over its noisy ways and was resting peacefully. I had expected to see the aluminum block sitting on the polished steel pan at the base of the device, being ground up or you know, eaten by little nano-bots or something. Pero nada.

"OK, I give," I said. "Where is the block? Your recycle thingy sent it to the Phoebe Ring around Saturn?"

"The Phoebe Ring? Excellent, Coop! I had no idea you were into astrophysics."

"Astrophysics? I'm afraid not, Augie. Although my mom dabbles in astrology if that counts. No, I wrote a paper on Galileo for science class last year. I found him fascinating and of course he discovered Saturn." I pointed at the recycle thingy again and said, "So answer my question. Where's the block?"

Augie turned his hands palm up.

"It does not exist anymore."

"What?"

"It doesn't exist anymore. At least not as a block of 7075 aluminum alloy. It was changed into pure energy, which was converted to electrical energy, which was then transferred to the storage device that provides some of the energy for this lab."

"So it's gone. Just gone?"

"Well, yes, it is *gone*. As you can see. Or not see." Augie giggled at his own little joke. "But it is definitely not *just gone*, as you say. All of it, one hundred percent, has been recycled as energy for later use."

"Well, that's amazing," I said. "You must be making a ton of money with this one."

Augie shook his head.

"No, this is a prototype. I still have a few kinks to work out. Efficiency, for instance. As I mentioned the block was one hundred percent recycled into stored electrical energy, but a fairly large amount of electrical energy was required to operate the re-cycler. The net gain was only about eighty percent."

"Only eighty percent," I said. I looked the bin over, then nodded. "Yeah, you gotta fix that for sure. And have you thought about maybe getting rid of the loud bang?"

Augie laughed.

"For sure," he said. Then his face lit up and he said, "Want to see my computer?"

Before I could reply, Augie was running toward the stairway. I chased after him and finally caught up on the opposite side of the lab, one floor up. Augie waited until I came near, then took his seat in front of the computer. The chair looked like it had been transplanted from the latest supersonic fighter jet, except that it was covered in what seemed to be purple leather. As soon as Augie planted his butt in the chair, it lifted him up and moved him forward. At the same time arm rests that had been folded out of the way rotated up and out. Augie rested his forearms on the padded arm rests and slipped his fingers, all ten of them, into recesses built into the ends of each rest. I looked around for a keyboard but didn't see one anywhere.

As the chair was delivering Augie to the proper operating position, the computer screen was busily coming to life with a soft glow and a ripple of numbers and images. I'm not talking about your average computer screen here, or even one of the fanciest big screens on the latest iMac. Augie's computer screen was a huge piece of curved glass that formed a complete semi-circle around him. It must have been three feet high and eight or nine feet from end to end.

I stepped over close to Augie's chair and put my head next to his. The images that had looked slightly distorted when I was standing further back snapped into sharp focus.

"Like it?" Augie asked with a grin.

Words just wouldn't come, so I nodded my head. You see a lot of futuristic looking stuff on television and in the movies these days, but here was the real deal.

"This looks even cooler than Tony Stark's computer in the *Iron Man* movie," I said.

"Mmm," Augie said, already involved in modeling a component of whatever he was working on. "I saw that movie, too. Actually, I tried the holographic approach long ago."

"You did?" I said, watching with fascination as he turned the component this way and that on a three-dimensional axis.

"Mmm," Augie said again. I was learning to translate "Mmm" as either *yes* or *I'm not really paying attention to you*. Apparently, it was the former because he said, "Yeah, but the problem is resolution. If you need extremely high resolution so that the small details aren't fuzzy, then you need a screen, not a projected image."

He did something with one of his fingers in the slots

on the arm of the chair and the device he was looking at jumped in magnification. Once, twice, then three, four and five times. With each zoom in, the details stayed sharp and focused. The folks at NASA or 3M would probably pay a fortune for a computer like that.

"What's that you're working on?" I asked.

Augie clicked the zoom function back to show the whole object.

"This is going to be an artificial larynx," he said. He flipped it and rolled it a couple of times as he inspected the thing. Then he added, "After I solve a few design flaws."

If this invention was anything like the others Augie had shown me, it was probably going to benefit somebody whose real larynx had been damaged beyond repair. I put my hand to my throat and tried to imagine this thing implanted in me.

"A bit large, isn't it?" I said.

Augie looked up at me from his fancy chair and smiled.

"Yes, actually it is a bit large," he said, "but the final version will be smaller." He turned his attention back to the computer and started closing things down. Augie put his baby to sleep and we returned to the house, where I discovered that driving was not Bart's only talent. We feasted on BBQ baby back ribs that must have been smoking all afternoon. Maybe in the part of the house that had once been a morgue, although I once again tried to put that thought out of my head.

I biked home later, thinking that ordinary homework – a history chapter on the War of 1812, ten algebra problems and a one-page essay on the life and times of Charles Dickens – suddenly seemed . . . superfluous.

# Chapter Five

SINCE I WAS a newcomer to Anacortes School, every teacher wanted to spend some extra time with me. That kind of special attention was one of the reasons my mother arranged for me to come here, so I couldn't complain. But it meant that sometimes I was tied up with other people and had to watch over Augie from a distance. I figured he was safe in class and just needed a guardian angel before and after classes started, and during lunch.

So Tuesday found me sitting in the cafeteria across from Mr. Pittman, the biology teacher, combining lunch with a "get acquainted" meeting. He was talking and I was listening with half an ear, since I had most of my attention on the next table, where Mika and Augie were sitting. Augie was facing away from me and Mika was facing in my direction. I don't think they were even aware I was in the cafeteria because they were involved in an intense conversation.

At least I think they were conversing. They weren't speaking; not words anyway. I think they were using sign language.

My trouble sensing system was on high alert because

every school cafeteria I've ever been in is a prime ground for bullies. I believe we should all be free of bullies everywhere, but . . . some idiots just can't stand anyone different from themselves and you'd have to go a long way to find something more different than *Augie the Brain* and *Mika the Indian Princess* conversing in sign language in the lunch hall.

Sure enough, George Banner came lurching up behind Mika, splint still stuck to his schnozzola. This time he was trailed by a pair of sidekicks armed with even less brains than himself. Banner hadn't seen me, so he thought he was home free. He started harassing Augie and Mika while his pals encouraged him. I gave Mr. Pittman a nod and a *yessir I understand* to keep him rolling, then I focused a hard stare on the sidekick nearest me, who I dubbed Sidekick #1.

Have you heard that saying, "I felt his eyes on me?" I've found that it actually works more often than not. Maybe it's a survival mechanism. I used my eyes now to bore into the feeble brain of Sidekick #1. In about two seconds he gave a little jump and looked right at me. I held his eyes. Down low, where Mr. Pittman couldn't see it, but the pal could, I pounded my right fist into my left palm. Sidekick #1 gulped, blinked and tugged at George Banner's sleeve.

Irritated, Banner looked down at the guy and said, "What?" Still holding onto Banner's sleeve with one hand, Sidekick #1 turned and pointed at me with the other.

When Banner finally saw me, I smiled and touched my own nose. Three times, in case he was slow to get the message.

I guess Banner could read sign language too, because he got my message all right. He spun on his heel and marched off, Sidekick #1 looking back with relief and Sidekick #2 wondering what the heck was going on.

I tuned in to Mr. Pittman again and found that I hadn't missed anything important. After we finished eating lunch he left, and about the same time Augie headed off for his next class. I slipped across to Mika's table. She smiled at me in a friendly way, clearly remembering me from the fencing match. She extended a hand toward the seat Augie had just vacated.

I sat and found myself tongue-tied again. Talk about feeling someone's eyes on you. That girl had eyes that hypnotized me in an instant. Finally I managed to say, "Hi Mika, I . . . ah . . . I noticed you and Augie signing to each other earlier. I was just wondering, why did Augie learn Indian sign language?"

Mika smiled – which made my heart jump a little – then she said, "Why did *Augie* learn to sign? Does that question mean that you assume *I* already knew how to sign because I am an Indian?"

"Well . . . yeah," I said.

Mika shook her head and said, "I have an aunt who was born deaf. I learned to sign from her."

"Sorry," I said. "Sometimes I'm a clueless ignoramus."

Mika shook her head and giggled.

"Coop, you're confused, not clueless."

I laughed with her, glad that she hadn't been insulted by my ignorance, and said, "That's my normal condition since I met Augie. Enlighten me, please."

"OK," she said. "You're thinking about the sign language developed by the Plains Indians. It was not used to communicate with deaf people, but for trade. You see, the various tribes all spoke different languages, or at least different dialects, so they needed a way to communicate with each other. So they could trade with each other for food, horses, weapons and such things. The system they developed is called Plains Indians Sign Language or sometimes Native American Sign Language. Augie and I were 'talking' in American Sign Language or ASL."

She flashed a series of finger and hand signals at me.

"That means *are you with me so far?*"

I flashed back a sign I had seen Augie use a number of times as I had "eavesdropped" on their conversation.

"*Yes.*"

"Very good!" she said. "Now, you mustn't confuse ASL with ISL."

"ISL?"

"Indian Sign Language," she said, her amusement plain in the way she smiled. "But the Indian in ISL refers to India, the large country with mega-millions of people in it. You know, the one on the other side of the globe?"

I whacked the palm of my hand against my forehead. At this rate I was going to develop a flat spot up there.

"I suppose there's a German Sign Language and a French Sign Language too, then."

"Actually, sign language is supposed to be universal. We use a symbol to represent a word or an action, so the symbols should be the same for everyone. But . . . there is actually a British Sign Language, and it's different than American Sign Language."

I rolled my eyes and Mika laughed.

"OK," I said, "It's more complicated than I thought, but I think I've got it. You and Augie were talking in American Sign Language and that's used by most people who can't hear for one reason or another."

"Right," Mika said, "although technically we were communicating, not talking."

I had to laugh again. How many mistakes can one guy make in a simple conversation?

"Well, you two were certainly *communicating* intensely. May I ask what it was about?"

"Of course, Coop," Mika said. "I was telling Augie about something that happened during the Lummi Nation Canoe Journey last July."

"Canoe Journey? You mean like birch bark canoes?"

"Oh no. A Lummi canoe is carved from a single log and is propelled by eleven paddlers."

"Eleven!"

"Oh yes. My ancestors have been traveling these waters for hundreds and hundreds of years, Coop. The annual canoe journey is a way to commemorate our Salish Sea heritage by inviting all the tribes in this region to join us. Last summer, nearly a hundred canoes crossed Hale Passage and came ashore at the Stommish Grounds on our reservation. You know where Lummi Island is, yes?"

Fortunately, I'd done a little homework after meeting Mika for the first time yesterday, so I knew the Lummi Nation owned Lummi Island and that the island was just north of Anacortes. I pointed in that direction and said, "Of course, right over there. Near Bellingham."

"Excellent Coop! So I was telling Augie that an orca harassed one of our canoes, which was highly unusual."

"I can imagine," I said. "I've never heard of an orca

going after any kind of boat. At least not one that wasn't harassing it first."

Mika nodded quickly.

She said, "And of course no Lummi Indian would do something like that. No, this canoe was just practicing their sprints when the orca showed up."

"What did it do exactly? Ram the canoe?"

"No, that's another weird thing. This orca surfaced right in front of the canoe, going very fast in the opposite direction. Then it passed down the starboard side of the canoe, very close to it, hitting every paddle with its dorsal fin."

"You're kidding!"

She shook her head. "Serious. It used its dorsal fin like a weapon, knocking the paddles out of everyone's hands. Two of the paddlers suffered broken wrists."

She paused and cocked her head, remembering something else about the incident.

"Augie was very interested in the incident, now that I think about it. He asked a lot of questions and walked away in a distracted fog."

"Is that unusual with Augie?" I asked.

Mika giggled.

"Oh no," she said. "That's typical Augie Sweetwater, for sure."

"Well, the whole thing sounds amazing," I said. "No wonder you and Augie seemed to be flashing signs at a frantic pace."

Mika paused for a moment and regarded me thoughtfully.

"Would you like to learn to sign, Coop? I can teach you too."

"Yes!" I said, "That'd be fantastic."

I shut my enthusiasm down a bit when I remembered that Mika's last pupil was Augie, the kid with more brains than ten Coops.

"Fair warning," I said, "I'm going to be harder to teach than Augie."

Mika shrugged.

"Augie is Augie," she said.

"Yeah, I'm beginning to get that," I said. "I suppose he could have taken up signing on a whim and mastered it overnight."

"On a whim?" she said, reflexively pulling back the way people do when they hear something that is both surprising and disagreeable. "Oh no. I think you have much to learn about Augie Sweetwater, Coop. He never does anything on a whim. Augie is the most focused person on planet earth."

"Then why did he learn to sign?"

Mika gave me her mysterious Indian look, which is difficult to describe if you haven't seen it yourself, but I can tell you it involves a devious smile and hooded eyes.

"I'll let Augie tell you about that himself," she said.

# Chapter Six

I HAVE ONLY known him for a few days, but I can safely say this about Augie: life around him is never dull. Most of us have routines, and routines collect dullness like boat bottoms collect barnacles. We go to school or work, eat, watch TV, sleep and repeat. Now and then we throw in something fun, like sports or movies or shopping. But the beat goes on and it's mostly the same, day-to-day and week-to-week.

Augie didn't have a routine. I don't think he ever had one and I'm willing to bet he never will. You could probably say that it was because of his astounding brain power, right? How could you get stuck in a rut with that kind of IQ? Or maybe it was because he's rich. When you're not scratching every day for food and shelter, it was easy to gallivant through life. I don't think either of those are why Augie's life was so exciting. I think it was because even though he was only eleven years old, but he led a dynamic life, not a passive one. For Augie, one thing always led to another.

The sign language thing is a good example. Taking

Mika's advice, I sat with Augie at lunch on Wednesday and asked him why he took the time to learn sign language. Augie pushed his glasses back up on his nose and peered at me for a moment through the thick lenses.

"Well, to speak with Leo," he said as though that explained everything.

"Oh, I see," I said. I didn't see, but my mom often used that phrase out of politeness, so I gave it a try. Politeness didn't prompt Augie to elaborate on his previous answer, so I did a little elaborating of my own.

"Who is Leo?" I said.

Instead of answering, Augie checked something on his ubiquitous iPad, then told me to come over to his lab at seven thirty that evening. I showed up on the dot, having no idea what to expect. What happened was that Augie introduced me to Leo.

Well, that's his nickname. His real name is Galileo. No, scratch that. I found out later that it was Mika who had named him Galileo; Augie had later shortened it to Leo. In any case, Leo's real name was unpronounceable. Literally. Unless you happened to be a dolphin. Like Leo.

According to Augie, one day at high tide Leo simply swam into the water channel that was cut into the lab from Fidalgo Bay. When the tide turned and the water in the lab was cut off from the bay, Leo stayed. According to Mika, this encounter was planned by the universe. Because why else would a dolphin with a badly damaged tail swim right up to the one inventor in the world smart enough to fix it?

Leo was in the cut again since it was near enough to high tide, which explained what Augie had been doing with his iPad earlier – checking the time of the next high tide in Fidalgo Bay. Inside the lab, the cut looked kinda like a long, narrow pool; a bit too wide to jump across, but long enough for swimming laps. At high tide, like now, the water was nearly level with the concrete floor of the lab. It looked considerably deeper than I had thought the first time I'd seen it; deep enough to jump in without touching the bottom. I guess Leo could sense the vibrations, because as we approached he launched himself into the air. I think he must have made it ten or twelve feet straight up. At the top of his flight, he looked directly down at me. Yes, down. He was that high in the air. He seemed to hang there forever – of course it was only for a split second – then he gave a high-pitched squeal, flipped onto his back and dropped back into the water with a splash that soaked us both.

"He always does that," Augie said as he wiped saltwater from his face, "even though I've asked him to be more considerate. He says that water is sacred to dolphins. What we call playing, they call showing affection and respect."

I wiped my own face and didn't say anything. I was still thinking about what I had just seen. I plan to study marine biology in college, and I'm fascinated by dolphins and whales. I'd already learned quite a bit about the marine mammals in Puget Sound from being out on Kevin's charter boat last summer. I admit I'm not an expert, but I know that other than seals, you were likely to see three other marine mammals around here. First off, there are the orcas. We call them killer whales, but they're not like blue whales and humpback whales. I think of them more as exceptionally large dolphins with a ton of teeth. Anyway, killer whales are what all the whale-watching boats in Anacortes and Friday Harbor are about. Less common are the

Dall's porpoises; fast, graceful and sporting a black and white paint job that looks like they copied it from the orcas. Third down on the list is the little harbor porpoise, a darkish gray, relatively shy porpoise.

Leo was clearly none of the above. I was almost certain that he was a bottlenose dolphin, except that bottlenoses are California critters, at least as far as the west coast of the US goes. I glanced at Augie and pointed down at the dolphin, now grinning up at me.

"But that's a bottlenose," I said. "They don't live around here."

Augie shrugged.

"Why not?" he said.

"The water's too cold, for one thing," I said.

We both looked down at Leo, who began lolling on his back in the water and not showing any sign of discomfort.

"Leo doesn't seem to mind," Augie said.

I knelt down to get a closer look. The dolphin brazenly stayed right where he was and looked back. His grin got even bigger and I could plainly see his teeth. Clearly, he hadn't come this far north to see a dolphin dentist, because they looked clean and sharp.

The dolphin made a noise that sounded like a cross between a giggle and a squeal, with some weird clicking mixed in. Then he flipped his head down and lifted his tail up. Somehow, he managed to stay almost motionless, half in and half out of the water.

"Leo must like you," Augie said. "He's letting you look at his new tail."

I wasn't sure that getting soaked and laughed at was a reliable sign that you've got a new friend, but I had to admit that Leo's tail was pretty amazing. The entire fluke – that's the big fin at the tail end of a dolphin – was bright yellow. I leaned over even closer. Now as I said, I'm no expert on marine mammals, but to my eye this fluke was not only yellow, but it was considerably larger than the flukes of most bottlenose dolphins Leo's size. Plus, the yellow part of his body extended up along Leo's peduncle. Kevin had made a habit, from the beginning of his entry into the Cooperlick family, of making every trip on his boat a learning experience. He's a good teacher and I love being out on the water, so I didn't mind. One of the things Kevin taught me was that the peduncle was the back end of a dolphin's body, where it tapers down to the fluke.

Augie knelt down next to me and reached a hand out. He gently grabbed hold of Leo's right fluke and pulled him over to the edge.

"Leo came to me with a severe injury. He had been attacked by an orca and lost most of his tail. It had been so bad, I'm still not sure how he was able to swim into the boat channel here."

Augie ran his finger along the trailing edge of Leo's fancy new fluke. Leo twitched a bit, like a kid getting tickled.

Peering closely at the yellow appendage like he was admiring his own handiwork, Augie said, "I invented this nano-fluke for him. With Bart assisting, I grafted it on to Leo's body."

"Nano-fluke," I repeated. "What's a nano-fluke?"

Augie let go of Leo's tail and Leo flipped himself upright. Augie grabbed my arm as he stood, forcing me to stand with him. Leo did the dolphin version of treading water, using his flukes to hold himself upright in the same spot. Augie pointed straight up, using the full extension of his arm and index finger. Leo immediately rotated himself over and disappeared underwater.

Now I should remind you at this point that Augie's lab is a converted lumber mill. One distinctive feature of this particular mill is its high ceilings. I haven't measured them personally, but when you're moving logs around all day you would necessarily want a little extra clearance overhead. I've seen photos of railroad cars bringing logs to the mills around here and photos of logs being floated in by water. The shortest looked to be at least ten feet; the longest twice that. So I'd venture to say that the ceiling in here must be three times as high as the ceiling in most houses. I'm telling you that so you can imagine my astonishment when Leo burst out of the water, launching himself high enough to touch that ceiling with his nose. Or his beak. Kevin would be disappointed, but I forget which was the proper terminology.

Augie wisely stepped back, but I was so enthralled that I stood right there by the water. Any parts of me that Leo hadn't soaked the first time got baptized when he splashed down from his spectacular jump.

When Augie and Leo both finished laughing, Augie said, "Leo's fluke is made of carbon fiber invested with thousands and thousands of nano-bots."

I nodded, mostly to let Augie know I was listening. So far, I didn't understand anything. I guess Augie could see that unhappy fact on my face, because he sighed like a kid whose dog refused to learn even the simplest trick.

"If you will recall," he said in a voice remarkably like my sixth-grade math teacher, "I introduced the concept of nano-bots when we talked about the bullet proof shirts I invented." Augie reached out and fingered my sleeve. "Like the one you're wearing."

"Oh, yeah," I said. "Teeny-weeny robots. And they all pull at the same time.

"Mmm, yes," Augie said, "although I don't think you appreciate how small. How about this? Imagine you have a spoonful of vanilla ice cream . . ."

"Now you're talking," I said.

Ignoring my interruption, Augie continued, "And I sprinkled a hundred thousand nano-bots onto your spoon. It would just look like I added one small drop of chocolate sauce."

"OK," I said. "Now I understand the nano part. Small. Really, really, really small. But why does it help Leo if they all pull together?"

"Ah, now *there* is an excellent question," Augie said.

I did my best not to blush.

"These particular nano-bots are twice as smart as the shirt nano-bots. They not only pull together; they push and pull."

"Push *and* pull?" I said. "Like up and down on the fin?"

"Yes, exactly," Augie said. "The trick is Leo's fluke has a lot of them. When needed, they push and pull in unison. Not all at once, but in sequence, up and down the fluke."

"And Leo nearly goes into orbit."

Leo made some clicking noises and Augie nodded.

"Of course, the nano-bots only amplify Leo's strength," Augie said. "Leo thinks he could nearly reach the ceiling on his own."

I made a scoffing noise in my throat, which earned

me another splash of water from Leo. I could see I'm gonna have to keep a close watch on this particular marine mammal. That thought reminded me of something else.

"Kevin told me about a law called the Marine Mammal Protection Act. He said messing with dolphins, whales or seals could get you in a lot of trouble."

"That's true," Augie said. "But . . . if the dolphin comes to you, it's OK."

I thought about that for a moment. It made sense, especially if the dolphin decided to swim right into your lab.

"But Leo's a California guy, right? How did he get here in the first place?"

Rather than answer, Augie left the glass enclosed part of the lab where Leo's saltwater cut was located and crossed to a set of cabinets in the main area. He retrieved something out of one of the drawers, then came back and handed it to me. It was a hat, which I took, although I'm sure my face was one big question mark.

"Well Coop," Augie said. "Don't just stand there, put it on."

"A cowboy hat?"

Augie shook his head, which caused his glasses to slip. He pushed them back up on his nose with a gesture that seemed purely automatic.

"Two things, my large and skeptical friend," Augie said. "First, that is not just a hat. It's an Akubra, which is practically the official headgear of Australia. My mother bought it for me when we visited Queensland, ten years ago."

"Ten years ago?" I said. "You were what, a year old?"

"She was a planner," Augie said. "She figured I would grow into it."

I thought he might be pulling my leg, but his eyes were absolutely sincere behind the thick lenses of his glasses. I took a closer look at the hat. It *was* exceptionally well-made, being constructed of smooth felt in a deep brown color. There was a lighter colored braided leather band around the base of the crown. The hat seemed heavier than it should, so I made sure I had a good grip on it. If it was one of Augie's treasured gifts from his mom, I'd hate to be the one who dropped it in the water.

"Yeah, mate," I said, carefully adjusting the hat on my head. "It's bloody bonzer. Now what was the second thing you were going to tell me about this hat?"

Augie didn't bat an eyelid over my attempt at Aussie slang, but I couldn't tell if he didn't get it, or he got it and just ignored it. I was learning that talking to Augie was like that a lot.

"Second," he said, "there is a device built into the brim of that hat that will allow you to couple your mind to Leo's mind."

Augie said that as casually as though inventing a mind reading device was about as difficult as inventing a paper-clip. That was another thing I was learning about Augie: he didn't think he was any better than anybody else. The fact that he could invent brilliant things like a mind reading device you could conceal in a cowboy hat – excuse me, Akubra – was just part of life for him. The kid was really growing on me.

"Kneel down at the edge of the water and lean towards Leo," Augie said. "Unfortunately, the range of the coupler is fairly limited. Your head has to be about three feet from Leo's."

I did what Augie said, only feeling slightly silly as I knelt next to a grinning dolphin with a bright yellow tail while wearing an Aussie cowboy hat. I still had a faint suspicion that this whole event was being recorded on hidden cameras to be played later for the amusement of the entire world. Or at least everyone at the Anacortes School.

"Perfect!" Augie said. "Now, you've got to understand that you won't actually be able to read Leo's mind. At least not like a Hollywood movie. You won't hear his thoughts in sentences or even words. You'll simply have an awareness in your mind of what is in Leo's mind. Remember he's a dolphin and you're a human, so you don't think the same way. It's going to be weird at first."

I said, "Right." But what I thought was, does he really think I'm going to forget who's the dolphin and who's the human?

Then Augie pushed a button that was concealed under the headband of the hat. He had told me it would be a little weird. Hah! It was being hit on the head with a flannel sledgehammer. A soft, fuzzy, man-that-feels-weird kind of sledgehammer. Then the world went blank and Coop was no more. I was a stranger in my own head, with one all-consuming thought:

I am a dolphin.

# Chapter Seven

**IN AN INSTANT,** I am not me. That Coop is gone. Gone, along with his homework, his four and a half fathers and his crush on the lovely young Indian princess with the confusing name of Michael. Poof! That Coop and all the things he wanted and worried about are gone. Like that Coop never existed.

I am Leo now and I am overwhelmed by . . . joy. I feel the joy from my powerful jump all the way to the ceiling. I still tingle with the exhilaration of that long fall back to the water. I feel the joy of zooming through clear blue water with my brothers and sisters.

When Augie broke the connection between Leo and me, becoming Coop again had been truly weird. Augie informed me later that I had been in contact with Leo's mind for about three minutes. I could not believe it at first, but Augie assured me that it was true. In my mind I had been a dolphin for . . . well, forever. The experience had been so powerful it had seemed like I had been born a dolphin and had been a dolphin all my life.

Now I felt so . . . so . . . clumsy. And overdressed. I had

to stifle the urge to strip off my clothes and dive naked into the cut. I settled for taking off my shoes and socks, rolling up my pant legs and sitting on the edge of the cut with my feet dangling in the cold water near Leo.

Augie sat next to me, with his feet out of the water and his ankles crossed. Leo sidled up close to us and held himself nearly motionless with effortless small movements of his enhanced tail. Augie was wearing his Akubra now, but he was signing to Leo in the language that Mika had taught him.

Without taking his eyes off Leo, Augie said to me, "After I fixed Leo up with a nano-bot augmented tail, we had been using the Akubra to mentally exchange images. It had been frustrating because as you have just experienced the process is kind of . . . overwhelming."

I just threw back my head and laughed. "You can say that again, my friend."

Augie took a microsecond to throw a quick smile my way, then he focused back on Leo.

"I'm translating for Leo everything you and I say," he said, "so that all three of us can follow the conversation."

Leo nodded happily. At least that's the way it seemed to me. That perpetual bottlenose smile must make it hard for Leo to look anything *but* happy.

"The beauty of the brain coupler," Augie continued, "is also its greatest problem. For the first time, we can actually experience what it's like to be a dolphin. Or an elephant, a rattlesnake or an eagle."

I said, "Uh, huh."

Man, I would love to have been there when our little Augster mind-melded with an elephant, a rattlesnake and an eagle. That must have been something to watch, especially the rattlesnake. No, scratch that. Augie at one with the elephant would have been my first choice.

"The problem is that there are intangible inter-species differences in thought processes."

"Umm . . . Augie," I said. "you need to translate that for me, too. But into plain English, not sign language."

To Augie's credit, I didn't hear the slightest note of exasperation in his voice when he said, "Human-to-human, the results are clear, and the experience is quite mild. Human-to-dolphin, or human to any other species, then problems arise because we don't think alike. And as you discovered, the experience can be overwhelming at first."

I nodded quickly and said, "OK, I get that. Leo's life was light years different from mine. Like that apples and oranges thing."

"Yes," Augie said, "apples and oranges would also have a difficult time communicating."

After Augie signed that to Leo, both of them bent over laughing. I blushed a nice deep shade of red right then. Around here, if you don't think before you open your mouth, you end up the butt of a joke between a kid genius and a bionic dolphin. Augie reached out a hand to high five and Leo scooted over to offer his fin, so it was all in good spirits.

Augie took up his signing to Leo again and said to me, "You are absolutely correct about one thing, Coop: dolphins and humans see the world from different perspectives; therefore they have very different experiences. But we also communicate our thoughts about our experiences in different ways."

"Oh yeah," I said, "we talk; dolphins use sonar."

"Basically, that's true," Augie said, "although humans use vision, hearing and touch to communicate as well. Dolphins use sonar, echo-location and vision too." Augie paused to flash a quick glance at me. "Dolphins are far better communicators than humans," he said, "partly because their methods of communication convey so much more information than speech."

Leo laughed and nodded, even though Augie wasn't finished with his explanation.

"Because humans and dolphins live in different worlds and communicate about our experiences differently, we also form our thoughts differently. On top of all that, the brain waves that we project when we have those thoughts differ in frequency and modulation."

I thought about what Augie had just said, picturing a dolphin in my mind. I could imagine the dolphin's smooth skin and sleek body. Suddenly I realized what was missing: ears! Dolphins don't have ears like humans, so even if Leo could understand words, he couldn't hear them.

"So Mika suggested sign language as a way to improve communicating with Leo," I offered.

"Exactly!" Augie said. "It was a brilliant suggestion. We started by showing Leo the gestures of sign language, along with the corresponding photos. Sometimes Mika even acted out things like eating, jumping and sleeping."

"How long did this take?" I asked.

"Two years," Augie said offhandedly.

"Two years!" I said. "You started when you were nine?"

Augie gave me the *what did you expect* look, which I'd already seen quite a few times and I'm sure I'd be seeing a lot in the future. The extraordinary is ordinary to Augenblick Sebastian Sweetwater.

"Teaching Leo sign language vastly improved our communication," Augie said. "Now Leo watches my hands and samples my thoughts, then sends his answers back by way of the Akubra device. It's still somewhat crude, and I have an idea for improving it, but for now this will have to do."

"Incredible," I said. "Would you ask Leo why he left California?"

Augie obligingly put the question to Leo, who thought for a moment. Augie received the mental message with his eyes closed and then spoke it out loud for me.

"Ocean warmer everywhere."

Leo apparently projected another thought, then let Augie translate it to English and say it to me. This same *thought/translate/speak* method continued for each piece of information.

"Fish go."

"Not have enough to eat."

"Much better here."

"Too many orcas here."

Then in an afterthought, Leo added, "Orca eat salmon . . . mostly leave us alone."

Did Leo just tell me the orcas *mostly* leave them alone? That's kind of like finding out that the night monsters are real, but they *mostly* stay under the bed.

# Chapter Eight

I'D BEEN AT the Anacortes School for less than a week when it got boring. No, I shouldn't say that. I had some great teachers, especially Miss McLean in World History. Yes, she was exceptionally good looking, but that was just icing on the layer cake of learning. She brought history to life and you wouldn't find anyone nodding off in her class.

The problem with school was that now it had to compete with . . . *The Amazing World of Augie Sweetwater and His Incredible Inventions.* How do you focus on determining the length of the hypotenuse of a right triangle that has a base of seven point three inches and a height of thirteen point six inches when you would rather be chatting with *Leo the Cyborg Cetacean*?

I plodded my way through Thursday. Then Friday finally rolled around, not a day too early for me. Dad One was coming to visit for the evening and I was looking forward to introducing him to Augie. I wanted him to meet Mika too, but she had already agreed to help on her uncle's boat after school.

My dad arrived in time to pick me up at school, which

raised my status with most of the other kids considerably. Before, I was just the new guy. The fact that I had become the principal's appointed protector of someone they labeled the world's geekiest geek hadn't helped much. But after I was picked up by a Seattle detective who could be mistaken for Matt Damon's older brother and driven away in an unmarked Dodge Charger that was hopelessly marked as a cop car by a forest of antennae, I was golden.

Dad gave me his usual manly handshake by way of greeting. Then he hit the gas and left about a foot of rubber in the school parking lot, which naturally added to the luster of my new golden-ness. We drove straight to Augie's, getting there just as Augie and Bart were climbing out of the Mercedes. After the usual introductions, we admired each other's rides. Cars didn't seem to be Augie's thing, but I got the distinct impression that Bart would have loved to get behind the wheel of something like that Charger with its big wide tires and gobs of horsepower. After a long, wistful look at the car, he steered us inside and got us seated in the living room while he rounded up some refreshments.

I'd told my father about some of Augie's inventions and could see by the way he kept surreptitiously eyeing Augie that he could hardly believe this kid was a master inventor. Bart noticed it as soon as he returned with a tray of drinks, chips and dip, so he jump-started the conversation after he sat down.

"Coop tells us you're a detective," Bart said to my dad.

Dad nodded as he picked up a glass of Coca-Cola.

"Thirteen years now. I worked vice – mostly drugs – for the last ten years, but it started to get to me, you know? Too much grief and too many just plain seriously bad people."

Augie seemed fascinated and Bart seemed sympathetic.

"What are you doing now Detective Cooperlick?" Augie asked.

"I run a small group – only five of us – that investigates missing persons."

"Can you tell us about your cases?" Bart said.

"Well, not specifics, but I can tell you that the state of Washington has one of the nation's highest rates of missing people. We have over five hundred open cases."

"Really?" Augie said. I could tell from his voice that the conversation had quickly passed the boundary between polite chitchat and genuine interest.

My dad nodded.

"Some are cold cases that may never be solved. We put our greatest effort into new cases where the victim is most likely to be in danger. Unfortunately, most of *those* cases involve children."

"How many cases do you handle at one time?" Augie asked.

"I can't give you a solid number, Augie," my dad said. "But . . . dozens."

In the silence that followed that dismal bit of information, Augie looked distraught for some reason. Since good detectives don't miss much and my dad's one of the best, he sensed that Augie might have a problem related to his work in missing persons.

"People call our office all the time to report missing persons," he said. "Fortunately, most of the time the missing person is found unharmed. In the US, more than 90% of children reported missing are found alive."

Augie's head came up. I thought he had a distinctly relieved impression on his face. So did my dad apparently, because he quickly added, "Of course the first few hours are crucial in the investigation, especially if a child had been abducted. We're more successful if we have enough information to act quickly."

Augie's happier face clouded again.

"Do you know someone who's missing, Augie?" my dad asked gently.

Augie regarded my dad silently for a moment, unsure about whether to say something. To solve his dilemma, my dad said, "We always encourage people to call if they're worried about someone. I make sure that none of the detectives in my office complain about wild goose chases."

Augie looked directly at my dad and seemed to find reassurance in his eyes. He gave a small nod and said, "I have a friend who was supposed to contact me two weeks ago, but I haven't heard from her."

"What's her name?" my dad asked. His manner had grown serious and I could imagine him mentally opening a case file on Augie's friend.

"Shizuko," Augie said, "Shizuko Li. She's eleven, same as me."

"Where does Shizuko live?"

Augie shrugged.

"She told me that she was originally from Shenzhen, but that her family recently moved to Kowloon."

"China?"

Augie nodded and my dad blinked a couple of times as he took in this new wrinkle.

"I take it you've never actually met your friend?" he said.

"Oh no," Augie replied. "We're online chess partners. She plays at a very high level."

"I see," my dad said. "Well listen Augie, I don't mean to sound like I'm brushing you off, but China is somewhat out of my jurisdiction."

Augie's head dropped just enough to show his dejection before my dad added, "However, one of the detectives on my team has family connections in Macao. I'm not an expert on Chinese geography, but I believe that's fairly close to Shenzhen. As soon as I return to the office, I'll brief her on your friend. She'll make an inquiry."

Augie nodded slightly, like he had hoped for more but was too polite to ask.

Bart cleared his throat and said, "I should begin preparations for dinner. Spaghetti and meatballs this evening. Augie, I'm sure you would like to invite both of your guests to join us?"

I noticed that Bart deftly made that last bit sound like both a statement and a question which got a quick glance of approval from my dad.

Augie brightened and said, "That would be excellent. I'm sure we have enough, right Bart?"

Bart laughed. "No problem, no problem at all," he said rising from his chair. "Why don't you three go over to the lab?"

My dad almost jumped to his feet. "Count me in!" he

said. "I'm embarrassed to say I leaned on my son's influence for this very opportunity."

So that's what we did. Leo wasn't around, and the tide was too low for him to enter the cut into the lab in any case, but Augie amazed my dad with his inventions right up until dinner. Bart's meatballs were delicious, and we left the table with that never-let-me-eat-that-much-again feeling. Dad had also scored one of Augie's bulletproof shirts, which he put on immediately. He was so enthralled with the shirt, it felt like he and I had switched roles. I was the dad and he was the kid who was going to sleep in his new shirt.

I had noticed after dinner that Augie was a bit pre-occupied and maybe a little sad, so I told my dad I'd stick around for a bit, then walk home. I didn't think the problem was Augie's online chess partner, because my dad had promised to get something going on that. I had a suspicion that it was about the whole father thing. My biological parents were divorced, but I considered myself extraordinarily lucky in the father department. I had five . . . well four and a half . . . and loved them all. Augie had none. Worse than none according to Mrs. T, the principal at Anacortes School. And the whole evening Augie had had a wistful look in his eyes whenever he caught my dad and I enjoying a father/son moment. Before I could ask him about it, though, Augie asked me if I'd join him on a small trip.

"I'll ask Bart to drive us," he said. "We're not going far, and we won't be gone long. We can drop you at your house afterward."

"Sure thing," I said. "Where are we headed?"

"To visit my mother."

# Chapter Nine

THE EVENING SHADOWS had deepened by the time the headlights of the Mercedes illuminated a gray stone gateway, with a wrought iron banner over the entrance that read *Anacortes Memorial Cemetery*.

Bart parked a short distance into the cemetery. He climbed out and opened one of the rear passenger doors, and both Augie and I slid out. He handed Augie a small but bright flashlight and said he would wait with the car. Augie and I walked off, his flashlight swinging circles of light on the smooth gravel of the narrow path that ran down the center of the cemetery. He stopped after we had walked perhaps twenty yards and aimed the flashlight at a tall marble memorial. It was the most elaborate grave marker I'd ever seen, complete with a pair of angels hovering on either side. The name Rose Evangeline Silver was etched into the front of the main stone with a flowery script. Augie swung the light to the side, where its beam found a marble bench between the gravesite and a small decorative pond. We sat together and he clicked the light off.

We sat quietly at first, our eyes gradually adapting

to the darkness. Some solar powered courtesy lights were spaced around the grounds on poles, so it wasn't completely dark. I could see the amber parking lights of the Mercedes near the entrance of the cemetery and Bart's face reflected in the light from the dashboard. I sat still and listened to the low croak of a couple of frogs communing with each other from the pond. It was nearly ten minutes before Augie broke the silence.

"My father is evil," he said.

I stirred and started to ask what he meant when Augie raised a hand that I could see in the gloom. I stifled myself and waited for him to continue.

"He's not a real person. Not like you and me. He has no conscience, no respect for life. He believes that he's the center of this particular universe and that the rest of us are only here for his entertainment."

"This particular universe?" I said. "There's more than one?"

I could sense Augie nod slightly.

"Many physicists believe that during the formation of the universe, that other universes were also created. In fact a physicist named Hugh Everett postulated back in the 1950's that there are an infinite number of universes. My father thinks he's the absolute king of the one he occupies, and that he can do anything he wants."

"But Mrs. T told me your father is locked up in a maximum security prison," I said, "and he'll be there for the rest of his life. How can he do whatever he wants?"

Augie scoffed.

"Prison is only a temporary inconvenience for him. He managed to hide away five million dollars before they caught him. He bribes guards to get special attention. He pays them to bring him cell phones that he can use once or twice without getting caught. When he has access to a smart phone, he might as well be in an office suite in Seattle. He can hire people to do whatever he wants."

"Bart told me that your father is always after you," I said. "What is it that he wants?"

"Two things," he said. "Both equally important to him, I think. First is control. He cannot abide me being free – not free as in not in prison, because I think he only views prison as a minor inconvenience. What he hates is me being free to do what *I* want, not what *he* wants."

Augie shook his head and blew a frustrated puff of air through his lips.

"The second reason he harasses me is money," he said. "The five million dollars that he hid away is a lot of money, to be sure, but it is not three hundred million. My father can't kill me to get the money, but he has a plan to kidnap me and force Mr. Kensington to pay a huge ransom to an offshore bank account that my father set up before they sent him to prison."

When Mrs. T had mentioned that Augie's mother had been worth three hundred million, I'd figured either she was exaggerating to get my interest, or that she was talking about money that existed in the past but was long gone by the time Augie's mom died.

"Wow," I said. Some supportive friend, right? Augie's psycho murdering father reaches out from behind the walls of a maximum security prison to screw with his life and all I've got is wow. Mrs. T would not be pleased. Before I could step up with something more helpful, Augie added to the pile of horrible things his dad did to him.

He said, "Remember those two men who attacked me the first day I met you?"

"The two bozos who burst out from behind the rhododendron bush and tried to kidnap you? The ones Bart hit with the Blue Blaster?"

"Yes, those two," Augie said. "But you stopped one of them and I won't forget it."

"My pleasure," I said, making a wave-off gesture.

"Anyway," he said, "you were right to call them bozos. They weren't particularly good at kidnapping, were they?"

"I kinda wondered about that."

"As you can imagine, my father can't be too picky about the men he hires. I'm always afraid that he'll send someone who succeeds one day, but in the meantime, I know why he keeps doing it even though they fail."

"Yeah? Why's that?"

"Because he knows that each time he sends someone, I'll have nightmares about him finally catching me." Augie said. "I'll wake up every night for the next week, drenched in sweat and shaking.

"Man," I said, "that's tough."

"I'll get through it," he said.

"Can't you do anything about the nightmares? Therapy? Medication?" I asked. What I was thinking at that moment though was *oh boy, this kid is way tougher than he looks.*

"We . . . that is the doctors I've seen, and myself . . . we've tried everything. In fact, that brain coupling device started out as an attempt to control my brain waves during sleep. To prevent nightmares."

"It didn't work?"

Augie sniffed. "Actually, it worked too well. It prevented *all* my dreams. But I discovered that we need to dream, at least now and then. If we don't . . . well, we get a little crazy."

I looked at Augie, sitting in the dark at his mother's grave. He looked a lot more peaceful than I would have, if I'd been facing a week of nightmares starring a serial killer.

"Thanks for telling me Augie," I said.

A few minutes later we returned to the car and Bart drove us to our separate homes.

## Chapter Ten

SATURDAY WAS FILLED with glorious sunshine, gentle breezes and a blue sky that made the snow-covered peak of Mount Baker pop against the horizon. It was the kind of day that created lifelong Pacific Northwesterners. As we sat at breakfast, I told my mom about the cemetery visit with Augie, and about his constant fear of being abducted by thugs hired by his psychopathic prison-bound, yet long-armed parent.

She was horrified naturally, but then she offered a suggestion. At first, I thought she was crazy.

"You and your friend Mika should take Augie shopping," she said.

"Shopping?" I said. Traipsing around a mall for hours is my least favorite way to spend Saturday. I'd rather mow the lawn, and that's saying something.

"You said he dresses like a geek. Take him to your favorite store; get him a makeover."

"The REI store in Seattle?" I said, brightening a bit. Recreational Equipment, Incorporated is the source of all outdoor stuff for half the outdoor people in the State of Washington.

Mom laid a gentle hand on my shoulder to signal that I should pay special attention to what she said next. "Sometimes," she said, "something as simple as a new look in clothes can lead to a new outlook on life." With her free hand she picked up my cell phone that I'd left on the table. She held it out to me and said, "Call Mika. Call Bart. Get going."

I smiled and took the phone. Bart thought it was a splendid idea. As soon as I told Mika about the cemetery visit, she was on board.

Three hours later, Bart was driving the three of us, Augie, Mika and me, toward Seattle. Everyone but Augie was in on the scheme and we were having a hard time keeping him happy. Most people love surprises, but I was finding out that in some ways Augie was more like a fifty year old businessman than an eleven year old kid. I suspected Bart had to literally drag him out of his lab for this trip.

"Why did we have to drive all the way to Seattle for lunch?" Augie asked as Bart steered the Mercedes smoothly off the I-5 freeway at the exit for Stewart Street.

"There's an excellent café here," Mika said.

Since I was sitting in the front of the car with him and Augie was in the rear with Mika, Bart only had to turn his head a few degrees in order to wink at me. Instead of turning onto Stewart Street, he swung right onto John Street and then onto Yale Avenue a short block later. He glided up to the sidewalk in front of a lush grove of evergreens, a very unlikely bit of landscape to encounter just a stone's throw from the highway in the middle of Seattle.

Bart said, "I shall be nearby, Mr. Coop. Just call when you have finished *dining* and I'll pick you up right here."

He unlocked the doors with his button and we piled out. Augie looked around in confusion, but Mika and I each grabbed an elbow and we steered him quickly through the gate and up the stone steps.

At the massive wood door, Augie said, "REI? Recreational Equipment, Incorporated? But what about lunch?"

I pulled the door open, while Mika encouraged Augie inside with a firm hand on his back.

"They actually do have a café here, Augie," she said. "We'll grab something to eat after."

"After what?" Augie said as he looked around the huge store.

I looked too, because I always enjoyed being here. They had all kinds of hiking, biking, climbing and paddling gear, but the clothing selection was why Mika and I had hijacked Augie to REI.

He was dressed – as usual – in rolled-up brown corduroy trousers – baggy in all the wrong places – patent leather black shoes, scraped liberally around the toes, and a blue bullet proof t-shirt. His black leather belt was about a foot too long, so the end stuck out from under the shirt and flopped against his leg as he walked, which looked pretty comical since he was also continually pushing his heavy tortoise shell glasses back up on his nose. Kind of like someone trying to walk, rub his stomach and pat his head at the same time.

Bart had assured us that none of Augie's clothing was

sacred. I mean like a gift from his mother or something that he would object to changing.

"His mother, bless her, dressed him the way her father and her dear brothers had dressed," Bart had said. "The way they had dressed a century ago, that is. Augie still dresses that way because he hasn't given it a moment's thought. I believe he never will, so by all means do your best."

As we stood just inside the threshold of the store, Mika looked Augie over with a critical eye and said, "Let's start at the top with the shirt, and work our way down."

I nodded in agreement with her logic and we towed Augie to the youth apparel section. It was like trying to take a dog for a walk that doesn't want to go; you know how they'll simply sit and not budge no matter how hard you pull on the leash?

When we at last arrived, the REI person in charge took one look at Augie and murmured under her breath, "Oh, my." She glanced at Mika and me, discerned the situation with no difficulty and in a cheerful voice said, "A top-down makeover?"

We both nodded emphatically. Mika discreetly flashed the gold credit card that Bart had loaned us. The REI person introduced herself as Nancy, then deftly took over the makeover. Mika and I plopped ourselves on a nearby bench. Nancy carried on for the next hour, pausing only to look over at us now and then for a thumbs up or a thumbs down as Augie tried on a growing mound of clothing.

In the end a new Augie stood before us. If we'd been worried that he might not want to change his appearance, it would have been wasted mental energy. He was clearly delighted by his new look, and so was Mika. She leaped to her feet and scurried around him, oohing and aahing like crazy. I had to admit, he looked good in a plaid shirt in shades of blue and tan, with the bullet proof t-shirt just visible at the neck. Both shirts were untucked so Augie's bulletproof shirt could function as designed, but now a proper length braided leather belt anchored a pair of khaki-colored cargo pants around Augie's skinny waist. The cuff-less pants broke perfectly at the ankle, over a pair of water-proof walking shoes.

On the counter behind Augie, Nancy had already rung up the sales and packed everything into oversized REI bags. Seven of them. Nancy had apparently made arrangements for help in carrying everything, because two other clerks gathered up the bags and promised to deliver them to Bart at the car.

Mika finally settled down and came to a halt directly in front of Augie.

"There's one more thing," she said, dipping a hand into the purse she'd been carrying slung over one shoulder. She pulled out a small hard-shell case, the kind used to store eyeglasses. She opened the lid and held the case out to Augie. "Bart gave us a pair of your spare glasses. Coop and I scurried over to the Anacortes Vision Center earlier this morning and had the lenses mounted in another frame." She dipped her eyes and said, "We hope you like them."

Augie curled the fingers of his left hand into a loose fist and pressed it to his mouth. "No one . . ." he said through his fingers. His chest gave a little hitch and I thought he might cry. "No one has done this much for me since my mother . . ."

I laid one arm around his shoulders and held my other

hand out for the old pair of glasses he was wearing. He nodded gratefully and took a deep breath. He gave me his plastic tortoise shells and carefully slipped on the glasses Mika and I had purchased for him. They were titanium frames, but in a light bronze color; modern and graceful compared to his old glasses. Behind the counter I could see Nancy discretely giving two thumbs up.

I agreed. The glasses were the final touch and the difference was astounding. Augie was still Augie, of course. Clothes can never change the inner person, only the image the world sees. He was the same innocent kid with a brain that Leonardo da Vinci would have envied; a kid who was a magnet for bullies. But man, he looked great.

The three of us trooped over to the counter and thanked Nancy for all her help, then ducked into the café for a quick sandwich. Mika and I both noticed Augie pause for just a heartbeat to check his reflection in another handy mirror as we passed through the men's wear section on the way, but we only smiled quietly to each other. We didn't want to keep Bart waiting – he had insisted on staying with the car – so we ate without dawdling and headed for the door.

I had my hand on the door handle when a loud voice said, "Aren't you going to give us a demonstration Coop?"

I was hoping to avoid this, but Augie stopped abruptly and asked me, "Demonstration of what, Coop?"

Mika stepped up next to Augie and said, "Yeah, what?"

Opposite the main door, REI had an indoor climbing wall. It was a beautiful piece of work, very professionally made. And very challenging. I'd been here many times with dads one and two and had climbed it more times than I could remember. In fact, I owned the record for the fastest time to the top. Five point three seven seconds. Which was exactly what the REI staffer in charge of the wall, a very nice guy named Doug, told Augie and Mika when they asked what he meant.

"Come on," they both said, pulling me toward the wall, "show us." Now it was me that was acting like the reluctant dog.

I dragged my feet and said, "We've got to hit the road. We have a long drive back to Anacortes."

"It doesn't matter," Augie replied. "We have plenty of time."

"Besides," Mika said, "it's Saturday. There's no rush hour traffic."

"I don't have climbing shoes," I said. "I can't climb in these running shoes."

"We have a courtesy pair that will fit you right here in the bin," Doug said.

What could I do but give in gracefully? I'm not the sort to show off, but everyone enjoys having their friends see them excel at something. I sat down and pulled off my trail runners, then laced up the loaner climbing shoes while Doug explained to the others what the record involved.

"He's got to start right here at the bottom of the wall with one foot on the start sensor. As soon as he lifts that foot, the time starts. He climbs as fast as possible, but not straight up. See how the hand and foot holds are color coded? He's got to use all the red colored holds." He pointed them out, his hand moving zigzag but always up. "See there at the top, that big green button? When he pushes that, the clock stops."

I did a few jumping jacks and pushups to warm up, growing more and more self-conscious as my friends were joined by other staff members and curious shoppers. I dusted my hands at the chalk bag so that my fingers wouldn't slip on one of the holds and then I approached the wall.

Mika slid up beside me, raised herself up on her toes and whispered, "Set a new record, Coop. I know you can do it."

I was more aware of her warm breath in my ear than of what she said. What is it about girls that can get guys to do any fool thing they want? Whatever, I was determined to zoom up the wall like Spiderman in a web-blasting hurry.

Doug hooked me up to a safety line, made sure everyone was ready, then he said, "Go!"

I took off.

The spectators erupted into encouraging cheers, but I was focused on the climb. Right foot up, left hand up. Left foot up, right hand over. Brace the right toe on an impossibly small red knob, left hand stretching out high above. Left toe above my waist, throw the right hand up. Catch another even smaller red hold with two fingers. On it went like that, the crowd's noises a dull chatter in the back of my brain; sweat breaking out on my face.

Too long, I thought. Way too long.

One last hard push with my right leg, almost slipping off the last foot hold. My outstretched fingers slapped the green button and I nearly back flipped off the wall. The safety harness took my weight cleanly and Doug lowered me the floor. I was shaking my head already, trying to figure out what to say to explain my failure. Then I realized they were cheering. As soon as my feet touched the mat, Mika threw her hands around my neck and kissed me square on the lips. She hopped nimbly back before I could react and pointed to the clock.

"Five point three five!" she said. "A new record!"

# Chapter Eleven

**AFTER BREAKFAST SUNDAY** morning, I pedaled over to Augie's lab. Mika had called both of us first thing and said, "I have something for you guys to see." I had planned to leave my bike on the front porch at Augie's house next to the lab, but I discovered they were both waiting for me already, sitting together in the four-person swing chair that hung on the porch. The sun had already risen well above the Cap Sante hill off to the east of Augie's place and Mika's face glowed in the soft golden light that flooded onto the porch. My heart did a little stutter step as I propped my bike against the rail at the far end of the porch and plopped myself down in the seat opposite them.

When we'd finished with all our *good mornings*, Mika said, "You know there is a Lummi totem at the memorial site in Shanksville, Pennsylvania, right? Where United Flight 93 crashed on September 11, 2001?"

That was news to me, and I admitted that I didn't.

"Oh yes," she said. "Lummi totems are quite well known, because of the skill of our artists. The Shanksville totem was carved to honor the victims. A larger Lummi totem, with two poles and a crossbar, has also been placed at the Pentagon Memorial Grove in Washington, DC. That one's intended to both heal and honor."

While Mika was talking, Augie had already brought images of both totems up on his iPad. We crowded around to check them out and read the captions. They were impressive, to say the least. After Augie put the iPad away, Mika went on with her story.

"A few days ago, I was watching my uncle at work on his latest totem. Not the uncle with the boat. That's Uncle Jake. Uncle Thomas is the carver. Anyway, he doesn't like to be disturbed while he works, so I was very quiet. I started thinking about how something big and solid like a totem can represent something like healing and honoring. These are symbols that help us up here." She tapped the side of her head. "Symbols that calm our thoughts or perhaps direct them in the right direction."

She checked our faces to see if we were still with her. I'm not sure what assurance my face gave her, but Augie sure looked like he was interested, so she carried on.

"Later on, I did some research of my own on symbols that help us in our lives." She reached into a backpack that she'd placed by the swing before I arrived. Holding up a sheet of white paper with a single drawing smack in the center, she said, "Check this out."

It was a black and white line drawing; spider-like, with eight legs. Each leg had a different foot and to my eye the whole thing looked something like the elegant katakana symbols that form the Japanese alphabet. Augie had a different take, and as usual his was the right one.

"A compass?"

"Yes, a compass," Mika said, giving Augie a little mock bow to acknowledge his good guess. "But not just any compass. A veg vee seer."

"Veeg vee ver?" I said.

"Not quite," Mika said. "Veg vee seer. Try it again."

"Veg vee seer," I said, earning a quick nod of approval.

"Actually, it's spelled v-e-g-v-i-s-i-r, but you say veg vee seer."

"Where's it from?" Augie asked.

"Generally, it's considered Norwegian," Mika said, "but it's also found in Icelandic and Irish literature."

"But how can it be a compass?" I asked. "It looks more like a fancy needle for a compass. Don't you need a housing for it? And some oil for it to float around in?"

Augie said, "I think you're correct, Coop. I believe this . . . ah, vegvisir . . . was never an actual compass. It was merely a symbolic compass. Something to help you decide to go in a certain direction."

"Yes," Mika said nodding in agreement with Augie, "that makes sense."

She held the drawing up so that all three of us could see it, then pointed to the arms of the design.

"Each of these arms is unique. See? The symbols at the ends are all different."

Augie leaned forward and peered closely at the drawing.

He tapped the paper and said, "Eight arms, for the eight cardinal directions. On our compasses they would be labeled north, northeast, east, southeast, south, southwest, west and northwest."

"Yes, I see that now," Mika said. "In the ancient art-works of my people, the Lummi Indians, four principal directions are commonly illustrated. North, south, east and west." She cocked her head for moment while she thought, then Mika added, "I remember reading that the Cherokee Indians have seven sacred directions. North, south, east and west, of course, but the Cherokee also revere up, down and into yourself." She held my eyes for a moment, then slowly turned to Augie and said, "It's important to look into yourself now and then."

The way she speared me with her eyes, then shifted over to Augie, I guessed that Mika was letting me know she'd found the vegvisir to help Augie cope with his dad. When I told her about the cemetery visit, Mika had been horrified for Augie. I don't think she counted a quick shopping trip as adequate therapy. In any case, I figured Augie could use all the help he could get, so I jumped right in with Mika's plan.

"So, if the vegvisir is only a symbol, how does it guide you?" I asked.

"Good question Coop," Mika said, smiling at me radiantly now that I saw her intention. "The Vikings carved it on the bow of their ships. Some of them also made amulets in the shape of the vegvisir and wore them around their necks with a leather cord."

Augie said, "And the vegvisir was supposed to direct you, like a real compass?"

"Yes, but there's more to it than that," Mika said. "Wait until you hear what direction the vegvisir was supposed to provide."

She dug in the back pocket of her jeans and came up with a folded piece of paper.

As she unfolded it, she said, "Let me read this, so I get it right."

She found her place, cleared her throat and read, "This is from something called the Huld Manuscript, which is a collection of spells from Iceland from about two centuries ago."

She cleared her throat again, then said, "The wearer of this sign will not lose his way in storms or bad weather, *even if he does not know his destination*."

Augie looked like he'd been struck by lightning. After a moment, he picked up his iPad and tapped furiously. When he found what he was looking for, he held the tablet up for us to see.

"Look at this," he said. "You can get a vegvisir pendant. It even comes with a chain so you can wear it around your neck."

"Oooh," Mika said, pointing at one of the pendants. "I like that gold-plated one. The bronze one is nice too. It has that green patina, like an artifact that has been dug out of the ground after many years."

"That's my favorite," Augie said. "Why don't I get one for each of us? I'll have them sent directly to you. That way you can look them over first. If you don't like them, you can send them back."

"Really Augie? That's so sweet of you," Mika said.

She gave me another look and I was able to read this one instantly. In the space of one of Augie's favorite nanoseconds, Mika's glance said, "Mission accomplished." Maybe I was getting the hang of talking to girls after all.

## Chapter Twelve

**SAME OLD SAME** old was the name of the game for the next school week. I got a *B* on a history quiz, wrote a three page report on *All Quiet on the Western Front*, which was simultaneously depressing and terrifying, and gave Principal Treneger an update on *Augie World*. She was pleased with Augie's new look.

There was one unexpected but very welcome development. I tossed a football to George Banner while we were playing around after school. He was startled but managed to catch it. He stood there undecided for a moment, then threw it back. Nice tight spiral. We passed it back and forth for a bit, then he left. I got a smile out of him as he turned away, which proved that giving a dog a treat worked better than a smack on the backside.

The following Saturday, Mika won both of her matches in the Washington State Youth Fencing Tournament in Edmonds, taking the trophy in the Young Ladies 12-14 Year Division. After the event we spilled out of the auditorium in raucous good spirits, a large group that included seven members of Mika's family, plus Augie and me. We were all headed back to the Lummi reservation, where dinner and a congratulations party awaited, along with forty or fifty additional members of her happy tribe who hadn't been able to make it to the match. Two vehicles were already waiting at the curb for the hour and a half drive home: a white Chevy Tahoe with Mika's dad at the wheel and Augie's familiar black Mercedes.

Mika pointed at the Mercedes and her mom said, "Yes, of course dear. Ride with your friends. We're going to be crowded in the Tahoe anyway." Mom, who by the way was a stunning older version of Mika, pointed a finger at Augie and said, "Straight to the reservation, young man. No McDonald's drive-thru on the way."

The three of us ran for the Mercedes, Mika holding her trophy high over her head. I opened the back door and we piled in. Bart eased us away with his usual smoothness and I had no sense that anything was wrong until the doors locked with a loud, obnoxious thunk. They'd always locked before with a discreet, almost silent, click. Augie and Mika were still admiring her trophy as I looked wildly around the interior of the car. My heart sank when I realized that this Mercedes wasn't Augie's Mercedes. Worse yet, the inside door handles of this car had been removed.

I leaned forward, dreading what I'd see. Or rather *who* I'd see in the driver's seat. Whoever it was, he certainly looked Bart-like. Same height, same slender build and erect carriage. But definitely not Bart. The driver never turned away from the road as I looked him over, but another person raised himself up from where he'd been slouched out of sight in the front passenger seat and calmly met my eyes. He pointed at Augie and Mika, then indicated that I should get their attention. I poked Augie in the ribs with my elbow.

"Ow!" he said. "Coop, that . . . oh."

Mika finally saw what was going on and quietly slid her trophy to the floor between her feet.

Augie took the situation in as well. He took in a deep breath and leaned back against the seat. He pressed his hands flat against his thighs, effectively wedging himself in place. He exhaled after a long moment and dropped his shoulders. To me, his body language expressed resignation rather than fear. I could see that Mika read Augie's posture and expression the same way. She was watching him with curiosity on her face rather than anxiety.

In a flat voice Augie said, "Grogan."

The man in the passenger seat grinned widely, exposing blackened gums and large yellow teeth desperately in need of a really good dentist.

"Augenblick Sebastian Sweetwater," he said. "I believe we have some unfinished business."

"What did you do with Bart?" Augie asked. "Is he OK?"

The man Augie had called Grogan sniffed with exaggeration, then down his nose like he could hardly be bothered with such trivia.

"He's back at your place," he said. "Unhurt, so far. He'll stay that way and go free with the rest of you when I get what I want."

Grogan reached a hand over the seat and made a *gimme* motion with his fingers.

"Cell phones," he said. "Now."

Augie and I passed ours up. Mika had a little purse slung over her shoulder and was fumbling around in it.

"Don't bother trying to call 911," Grogan said, snapping his fingers at her. "This whole car is a giant Faraday box. I've rigged it so no cell phone signals go in or out."

Mika flushed, but immediately slipped her phone out and handed it over.

Grogan stacked the phones together, then passed them to the driver who stashed them in his inside jacket pocket. The driver, in spite of being not Bart, steered the Mercedes smoothly through traffic as we drove away from Edmonds and headed north on the I-5 freeway.

Mika leaned over to Augie, who was sitting between us, and whispered, "Augie, who is that nasty person and what does he want?"

Augie sighed, then he said, "Grogan is a partner of . . . no, partner is not accurate." He glanced up at Grogan who was talking softly with the driver and ignoring us. "Let's just call him a friend of a man I hope never to see again. Dr. Julius Underwood."

"Dr. Julius Underwood."

Mika said the name as a statement, but her eyes clearly held a question.

"Dr. Underwood is the founder of a company called Empire Concept Development," Augie said.

"Empire Concept Development," I said, with exactly the same inflection and facial expression as Mika. At this rate we'd die of starvation in the back of this Mercedes before we got the whole story out of Augie. I made a twirling motion with my index finger, the universal *Let's Get A Move On* sign.

Augie nodded and said, "Empire Concept Development is exactly what one might expect from their name.

They take an idea – a concept – and develop it into a working product. The concept may be for some object, like say a new kind of aircraft or weapon, but it may also be for something intangible, like a better way to organize a hospital or a supermarket."

"Sounds like a useful sort of company," I said. I paused for a second then added, "But you don't look at all happy about it."

Augie nodded slowly and said, "Correct. This would be a very fine and useful company except for one thing: the concepts they develop are mostly stolen."

Ah, I thought. Now I understood so clearly that I wouldn't have been surprised if a light bulb had appeared above my head and suddenly lit up the whole back of the car.

"Stolen from you," I said.

"Yes!" Augie said fiercely. "Julius Underwood is a thieving pirate."

I've never seen Augie so worked up before. I put a hand gently on his shoulder. "Wow, Augster," I said. "Don't give yourself a hernia. How did you get involved with this Julius guy anyway?"

I could feel Augie relax a bit, but only half a notch. He was still wound pretty tight.

"I used to work for him," Augie said.

"And he stole your ideas," I said.

Augie nodded, his face miserable.

"We had an agreement that my ideas, my inventions, would be my property. Mr. Kensington made sure that I was protected in that way. I never would have worked for Dr. Underwood otherwise."

"Um, why *did* you work for him Augie?" Mika asked.

Augie sniffed, then pulled a small rectangle of micro cloth out of his pocket and used it to clean his glasses before he answered. Glasses back in place, he sniffed again and said, "Dr. Julius Underwood is a brilliant scientist, no one would dispute that. I was flattered that he invited me to work in his lab. I didn't have my own at the time. And Dr. Underwood could work quickly to bring an invention from an idea on a computer to a reality. To a finished product, you know?" Augie shook his head. "I didn't have my Detroit company either. I was just plain ignorant."

Mika and I looked at each other, eyebrows high on our foreheads. Augie? Ignorant?

"It's true," Augie said. "I was a babe in the woods back then."

Mika and I both struggled to keep our faces straight. Babe in the woods? Back then? What about now?

"Anyway," Augie said, "Dr. Underwood wanted me to modify my brain coupler so that it could be used to control someone, not just receive mental images from them."

"That doesn't sound right," I said. "In fact, it sounds like a really bad idea. Wouldn't that be a crime?"

"Yes!" Augie said. "It would be wrong. And I told Dr. Underwood so."

"Good for you," Mika said. "What happened after that?"

Augie looked at his lap for a moment. I think he was probably re-living that time in his life. It didn't appear to be something he really wanted to do.

"He relented," Augie said, looking up again. "He said he understood and apologized for suggesting it in the first place." Augie took a deep breath and let it out slowly. "I left his lab three months later. On good terms, I thought. But I discovered later that Dr. Underwood had copied my prototype and stolen the original data files for the brain coupler from my computer."

I sat back in my seat, wondering how the fact that Augie worked for the underhanded-data-stealing Underwood had gotten us kidnapped by underhanded-Bart-stealing Grogan, when I finally put it together.

"Underwood gave Grogan the plans for your brain coupler," I said.

Augie shook his head. "Dr. Underwood never *gave* anything away in his life. He's the epitome of greed. I'm sure he *sold* the stolen prototype to Grogan."

Now we were getting to the heart of the story. At least if epitome meant what I think it did. I'd have to look that one up later.

I said, "Since Grogan has grabbed you, I take it this particular prototype didn't work, or at least not well enough, and he wants you to fix it."

Augie simply nodded. I could see he was tired of this whole thing. Who wants to worry all the time about being kidnapped and forced to help crooks or killers?

"Why would Grogan want the brain coupler?"

Augie said, "Grogan had always been talking about some get rich quick scheme, usually involving gambling of one kind or another. It's likely that his current scheme involves gambling too. I would bet that he thinks he can use the brain coupler to read the minds of all the players at a poker table and see what cards they are holding."

"Hmm," I said. "I could see where that might be

useful. You chill out until you know you're going to win, then you bet all your money."

"Yes, but you've seen how the coupler works. You've got to be in close proximity to each other, and you don't read actual thoughts. You see a state of awareness. What it's like to be that particular person or animal."

"Yeah, I got that from my experience with Leo," I said.

"There's one other limitation. I didn't mention it before because it made no difference to you and Leo, but any creature subjected to the brain coupler feels it." Augie tapped his head. "In here. They don't know exactly what it is, but they know something new is going on in their head."

I mulled that over for a minute, then I saw the problem.

"When the other card players feel someone peeking into their brains, they're going to know that someone is cheating."

"Exactly," Augie said.

"And they're not going to sit still for it."

Mika, who had been following our conversation, said, "That's the epitome of understatements."

# Chapter Thirteen

**WE RODE IN** silence the rest of the way to Anacortes. When the car was parked in the driveway between Augie's house and the lab, Grogan said, "Listen up. Maybe you're thinking I wouldn't hurt you kids, huh? Well, you'd be wrong, but it don't matter cause I got your man Bart tied up in the house with my other man. Bart's counting on your cooperation. Screw around with me and you'll never see him alive again."

He nodded at the driver, who pushed a button and the door locks thumped open. My spirits lifted with the locks. We were still at the mercy of Grogan and his driver, but at least we weren't trapped in the back seat of the car.

"Let's go," Grogan said.

We all clambered out. Grogan sent his driver to the house, to check on Bart and his second guy. Then Grogan marched the rest of us like a funeral procession to the massive door of the lab.

"Open it," Grogan said.

Augie shoved his hands into the fancy door lock, which hummed briefly as it analyzed his fingerprints, palm prints and heartbeat. The light over the door switched from red to green. Augie pulled his hands out, opened the door and led us into the lab. Grogan pointed to the nearest workbench and we gathered around it. Grogan reached into the briefcase he'd been carrying, pulled out a slim metal and plastic ring and tossed it on the table. Augie's personal brain coupler was hidden inside his Akubra hat, but I assumed this ring was an unadorned version made by Underwood. Or maybe the prototype copy Augie had mentioned.

Grogan dropped the empty briefcase onto the floor. He crossed his arms, stuck out his chin and said, "That one doesn't work. Make me twenty that will."

The three of us snapped our heads around to look at Grogan.

"Twenty?" Augie said.

Grogan smirked and said, "Didn't think I knew how that mind reader thing works, did ya? Well, I'm not going to use it on card players. I'm going to use it on the blackjack dealers. And my people don't need to know exactly what cards the dealers are holding. All they gotta know is how those card dealers *feel* about their hands. If the dealers are worried, my people will bet big; if the dealers feel confident, my people stay low. I'm going to hit twenty casinos all at once, so it don't matter if the card dealers sense something strange in their little skulls. Couple of big winning bets at each place and my people are out of there. I'll wait a week or so, then hit twenty different places. When I've worn out my welcome in the US, I'll move on to Europe."

Mika said, "It could work, you know. I've been to the Swinomish Casino out on Route 20 with my father. If you sat next to the dealer at a blackjack table, you'd be close enough. Cover the brain coupler with a loose-fitting hat, and nobody will see it."

Grogan's smirk grew even smarmier.

"Listen to your girlfriend, Augie," he said. "She knows I can pull it off. Now, get busy."

Grogan plopped himself down on the nearest chair.

"Do it, or your precious Bart is history," he said.

Mika and I moved up on either side of Augie as he stood by the workbench gazing forlornly at the prototype. All three of us were moving and thinking like zombies. Well, moving like zombies anyway cause I guess zombies don't think much. My brain felt like it had been replaced by a bowl of cold oatmeal, but I knew we needed a plan and we needed it fast.

"Augie," I said quietly, "how long will it take you to make twenty brain couplers?"

Augie stirred from his zombie reverie and looked up at the ceiling. I could almost see the gears working in his head as he made the necessary calculations. "One hour and thirty-seven minutes," he said.

"Really? That fast?" Mika said.

Like Augie and me, she kept her voice barely above a whisper. I glanced over at Grogan and was relieved to see that rather than focusing on us, he was looking around the lab. Who wouldn't be fascinated by Augie's high-tech Bat Cave?

Augie nodded at Mika's question.

"I have a new type of 3D printer," he said.

"Of course you do," I said. "Now, here's the real question. How long to make one real brain coupler and nineteen non-working replicas? Plus a nice case to hold them all?"

"Less than an hour," Augie said. "But why? As soon as he discovers the replicas, he'll have Bart killed."

"Hmm," I said. "We do need to avoid that. But see, Grogan doesn't know how your security lock works, right? You know, the one that opens the front door?"

"So?" Augie said.

I glanced at Mika and could tell that she was with me already, but sometimes Augie stumbled over the little gray cells in his own huge brain. I made a rolling motion with my finger to let Mika take it from here.

"Augie," she said. "What happens when someone who is not programmed into your lock sticks his hands into it?"

"The lock automatically slaps a set of steel handcuffs on . . . oh, I see," Augie said. "I'll build a special case for Grogan to hold his twenty brain couplers."

"Right!" I said. "Supposedly programmed to open just for him."

"But it locks his hands inside, so we have him trapped," Augie said.

"And then we trade him for Bart," I said.

That's what we did.

And it nearly worked.

# Chapter Fourteen

AUGIE SETTLED INTO his computer chair and made a few crucial changes to the latest version of his brain coupler; mostly taking out the working guts and substituting a bit of scrap metal to the innards so that the fakes would weigh the same as the real ones. Then he cranked up the 3D printer and started making copies. As fast as they rolled out of the printer, Mika installed the necessary switches and LED lights. They felt like the genuine article all right, and they twinkled impressively with the LEDs. But they didn't function at all. After the first ten, Augie stopped the printer.

Grogan, who had been sitting near the railing just keeping an eye on us, immediately rose to his feet and asked about the hold up.

"It's got to cool down for at least twenty minutes," Augie said, waving a hand at the 3D printer. "I'll make the box for them while we wait."

"The box? What box?" Grogan demanded.

"I designed a special box for the couplers," Augie said. "You don't want them to fall into the wrong hands, do you?

This box has two functions: it keeps them physically secure and it activates and deactivates them."

"What do mean, activate and deactivate?"

Augie gave a tiny little sigh, like he was dealing with a child.

"When you put the couplers in the box," he said, "they will automatically be recharged and deactivated. Then they'll stay deactivated and locked in the box until you open it."

"What if some other guy opens it?"

"That won't happen," Augie said. "Remember the way I used both hands to open the lab? This will work the same way. It will be programmed to read both of your palms and all of your fingers. Even the rhythm of your heartbeat. Nobody else will be able to open it. The couplers will remain in the box and stay deactivated until *you* want them, and only *you*."

"Underwood was right – you are a genius," Grogan said with an eager nod. "Do it."

Augie set to work again, working this time with steel sheets about an eighth of an inch thick. The waterjet machine cut pieces according to the design that Augie quickly drew up on his computer. Rather than take the time to set up one of his welding robots, Augie welded the box by hand. I could only shake my head as I watched him lay down a perfect bead of molten metal along each seam. This kid could do everything. Well, as long as it didn't involve fending off bullies. My money was on him owning the world one day.

About an hour and a half later, we had everything ready. The box was sitting open on Augie's workbench, loaded up with twenty brain couplers. The top unit was the real deal; all the rest were fakes.

Grogan stood there with his eyes wide open and glistening with anticipation. He picked up the top brain coupler, found the on/off switch and turned it on.

"This better work," he said.

"If you stand here with all of us, you'll get confusing signals," Augie said.

"Huh," Grogan said. "Makes sense, I guess. You and your friend step back. I'll stand next to the girl."

Mika shot me a worried look. I gave her a quick OK sign, down low where Grogan couldn't see it. Augie and I moved back, but I stayed as close to Mika as I dared. Just in case. Grogan nodded, then lifted up the brain coupler and settled it on his head like a crown.

Nothing happened for ten long seconds. Then suddenly Grogan grinned, and Mika cried out, "Oh, that's gross!"

"What?" I said, pulling Mika away from Grogan.

She shook her head and flicked her fingers like she'd just dipped her hands in a sack of squirming frogs. "Nothing really, just . . . gross. That man's brain is so gross."

"And you, little lady, are a delight," Grogan said.

He took off the brain coupler, switched it off and placed it carefully back in the box.

"OK, show me how this box works," he said.

Augie closed the lid. A green LED on the front of the box shimmered once and turned red. "It's locked now," he said. Then he pointed out the two openings on the front of the box. They were about six inches in diameter and about a foot apart. "You have to reach inside here," Augie said, "and wrap your fingers around the hand grips. The sensors will read your palm prints, fingerprints and pulse, then the box will unlock."

Augie stepped aside and held out a hand, inviting Grogan to give it a try.

Instead, Grogan pulled a small black pistol from his coat pocket. He pointed it at Augie and said, "You try it."

Augie raised his hands as though he could ward off bullets from Grogan's gun.

"It's programmed for your hands," he said. "Mine won't work."

Grogan reached a long arm out and grabbed Mika by the collar. He yanked her close and jammed the barrel of his pistol under Mika's jaw.

"Guess what, smart guy?" he snarled. "Your brain reader works just fine. Know what girlie-girl here had on her mind? She should have been scared, but the message I got when my brain was mixed with her brain was relief. She was about to get happy, so I figure you're about to spring some kind of trap. Now stick your paws in there."

"I'll do it," I said. I stepped up to the workbench before Grogan could object and stuffed both hands into the holes on the front of the box. As soon as I touched the grips, we all heard an audible CLACK! as steel cuffs grabbed my wrists.

Grogan shouted, "Ah hah!" and moved his gun toward Mika's forehead.

Desperation dumped a load of strength-giving adrenalin into my muscles. I got a solid grip on the handles inside the box, then I lifted and spun with all my might. I put my legs, back, shoulders and arms into it, like an Olympic weightlifter trying to set a record. The steel box came off the table like it was feather light and slammed into Grogan's jaw with a frightful, sickening crunch.

He fell straight to the floor. Way over balanced by the

momentum of the heavy box, I landed on top of him with my hands still locked inside.

I laid there for a few seconds, listening to my heart hammering away. It was still going *chooka boom, chooka boom, chooka boom* when Augie and Mika each took an arm and helped me stand up.

"Are you OK?" Augie said.

"Is he . . . dead?" Mika said.

"Yes and no," I said.

They both cocked their heads at me – I couldn't help but think of the way Principal Treneger did the very same thing every time I was in her office – and said, "What?"

I heaved the heavy safe onto the workbench and said, "Yes, I'm OK and no, he's not dead. He was breathing right into my nose down there, and it smells like he ate a dead squirrel. With garlic. And onions. Now, how bout we get my hands out of this device and put his into it?"

Augie tapped a code into a keypad on the front of the box and it relinquished its steely grip on my wrists. I moved it to the floor, then the three of us pushed and pulled Grogan's unconscious body over to the workbench. We put one arm on each side of one of the bench's metal legs and slid his hands into the box. Augie's metal trap grabbed his wrists with a satisfying *clack*.

"He's not going anywhere," Augie said. "I welded that bench together myself and bolted it into the concrete slab."

"We need to call the police," Mika said.

Augie shook his head. "There are no phones in here and Grogan's driver has our cell phones."

"We can use your computer. Contact them online," Mika insisted.

Augie gave her suggestion a moment's consideration, then said, "The Anacortes Police are not set up to take 911 calls online and not by Facetime or Skype. Even if we did manage to email someone at the police station and convince them that it was an emergency, I'm concerned that they might rush over with sirens and flashing lights."

Mika blew out a breath of air and looked down.

"Then one of the guys guarding Bart might shoot him," she said. She looked up and asked, "So what can we do?"

"Well, we've just got to free Bart," I said. "Grogan's guys don't know we've escaped. I can sneak over and take them by surprise."

"But what if they see you first?" Augie said. "They'll kill you."

I pinched a handful of my shirt and held it out. "I'm wearing my bullet proof shirt."

Augie shook his head. "What if one of them shoots you in the head? Or the leg?"

"Don't you have more of the shirts here?" Mika said. "We can cover his whole body except for his head with those."

"Yes!" Augie said. "An XXL will hang down below your waist and we can tape another oversized shirt around each leg."

"Um," I said, "what about that other part you mentioned? You know . . . my head?"

"I have that covered," Augie said, disappearing into one of the back rooms of the lab.

Mika and I stood there for a few moments in silence. I suspect both of us were still freaked by the whole thing. Kidnapped, threatened with a gun, and my brief but-oh-so violent fight with Grogan. Then Mika said in a serene voice as though we were waiting for Augie so that we could all go out for an ice cream cone and a walk along the bay, "Do you suppose he meant that pun when he said he has you covered?"

It settled my nerves, as she no doubt intended. There are times when this Lummi princess is far stronger than me.

"Intentional humor?" I said. "Our Augie?"

We both laughed at the thought and busied ourselves getting my t-shirt body armor duct taped firmly in place where it needed to be secure and hanging loose so that it could function as Augie had designed.

Augie returned after a few minutes – minutes that seemed like hours – with a simple baseball cap.

"Here," he said, reaching up to place it firmly on my head.

I rolled my eyes up to look at the bill of the cap, which looked ordinary in every respect. The cap itself, however, felt noticeably heavier than most that I'd worn.

"OK, maestro," I said. "I'm sure it's not just a hat. How's it going to keep my head from being shattered by bullets?" The danger of this rescue scheme was sinking in and I really didn't want my head shattered.

Augie said, "This hat houses a tiny generator that arranges the air molecules around your head into a solid shape."

"What kind of shape?" I said.

"Well, I didn't have much time, so it's a simple umbrella shape. But it extends from about a foot over your head down to your shoulders. As you move, the generator continuously adjusts. The net effect is an invisible umbrella that moves with you."

"So, my head is protected by air that forms a solid but invisible umbrella?" I said.

Augie blinked behind his glasses and nodded vigorously.

"But when you say the air molecules take on a solid shape, um . . . exactly *how* solid are you talking? Strong enough to repel bullets?"

Augie nodded again. Somewhat reluctantly this time I thought.

"I boosted the power output and focused the beam that shapes the virtual shield into a very tight pattern. That should be sufficient."

I had a lot of trust in Augie's inventions by now and I was fine with his explanation. Until he added under his breath, "I hope."

He reached up, pushed the button on the crown of the hat and quickly stepped back. There was a humming noise, then the hat felt like it got heavier. Augie used his fingers to find the edge of the virtual umbrella, then he made a fist and rapped his knuckles on it. He seemed to be knocking on thin air, but it sounded like he was knocking on a steel door.

"Brilliant, Augie," I said. "Thanks."

I picked up the gun that Grogan had been threatening us with. It was a black semi-automatic pistol. There was some information engraved on the barrel, so I held it up to the light. I discovered it was made by a company called Smith and Wesson, and that it fired 9mm bullets. I wasn't familiar with the gun and not absolutely certain how to use it properly. Augie saw my hesitation as I turned the thing over in my hands.

"Just a second," he said. He ran up the stairs to the second floor. I decided I wasn't going to use Grogan's gun no matter what, so I set it down. Then Mika and I waited, me feeling like I was about to go trick-or-treating in my costume of t-shirts, duct tape and invisible bulletproof umbrella hat. Augie wasn't back in just a second, but he clattered back down the stairs in less than a minute.

"Here," he said, holding out a Blue Blaster like the one Bart had shown me. Augie told me to grip it like a pistol. Unlike Grogan's pistol, it vibrated in my hand, then settled down in a gentle pulsing motion, almost like a hand massage.

"OK," Augie said, "you're ready to go. Remember, the maximum range is twenty feet. Aim for the torso, but any-where will work."

I thought the Blue Blaster would give us the edge we needed, so I put aside my misgivings about my so-called body armor.

"OK," I said, "here's the plan and it's simple: Mika goes around to the back and knocks hard on the door. That should divert their attention, while Augie opens the bio-metric locks on the front door. Then I run in and blast the blue blazes out of Grogan's partners."

Augie and I moved quietly to the front door while Mika snuck around back. Augie opened the locks, then we waited, scarcely daring to breathe. When we heard Mika pound on the back door, Augie opened the front door and I charged in.

Both of Grogan's men were standing next to the chair

where they had Bart tied up. Mika had created such a racket that they were both looking toward the kitchen when I came in behind them. I aimed the Blue Blaster at the guy on the left and pulled the trigger. He went down like a buffalo had been dropped on him. The guy on the right managed to turn part way around and pull a gun from his waistband. I blasted him too. He dropped the gun and fell next to his buddy.

I turned to Bart and discovered that he wasn't actually tied up; he was trussed up with even more duct tape than me. In fact, he was almost mummified from neck to waist with silver duct tape. A couple more wraps of the stuff around his jaw were keeping him from talking, but his outrage was plain enough in his eyes. I used my pocket-knife to cut him loose while Augie let Mika in through the kitchen door.

Mika called her parents, who took about one second to go from being mad at her to being relieved she was safe. They announced they would be here in twenty minutes.

Distraught was the only way to describe Bart. It turned out that someone who appeared to be a uniformed Edmonds deputy had approached him while he waited in the parking lot with the car. Explaining that a BOLO (be on the lookout) had been issued for a stolen black Mercedes S500, he had asked to see the car's registration. As soon as Bart had leaned over to fetch the paperwork from the glove box, the bogus deputy had injected him with a drug that had put him out immediately. He'd regained consciousness about two hours later, trussed up in the chair with a gun barrel in his ear.

"Never should have happened," he kept saying over

and over as he paced round and round after we freed him. "Never happen again."

Augie finally stepped in front of him, reached way up with both hands and turned Bart's face down to meet his own.

"I know, Bart," he said, "but it was as much my fault as yours. I should have looked more closely at the car before I jumped in. We'll have to work out a secret identification system, just for you and me. Perhaps a pair of tiny LED lights. We can install them under the fenders by the rear wheels, hidden unless you know where to look. They will be red by default every time the car is started. You'll have to change them to green so that I'll know all is well."

Bart blinked a couple of times, then straightened up and transformed himself back into the unflappable, always reliable Bart we all knew and loved.

Mika's parents actually arrived in thirteen minutes, thanks to police escorts from the Lummi tribal police, the Washington State Highway Patrol and the Anacortes police. After I called, my mother made the four minute drive from our house to Augie's in two minutes and planted a bunch of relieved kisses on my forehead. From that point, it was all cops and cleanup.

Nobody wasted any sympathy on Grogan. The paramedics revived him and stabilized his head and shoulders with a neck brace. Augie let him out of the steel box trap he'd rigged up, then the cops slapped their own steel cuffs onto his wrists and escorted him to the hospital.

Sure enough, Grogan's accomplices wet their pants as a side effect of being hit by the Blue Blaster. They were hauled away too; cuffed and smelly.

# Chapter Fifteen

MONDAY AT ELEVEN o'clock the Anacortes School PA system crackled a couple of times, then squawked so loudly that everyone in my math class winced and covered their ears. It buzzed a while before Principal Treneger's electronically disguised voice said, "Mr. Cooperlick, report to the principal's office after last class today."

I slunk as low as possible in my desk as all eyes turned to me. I'd gained a little notoriety after the George Banner broken nose incident and I could see everyone wondering just what the heck I'd done now. To make sure that my face was as red as possible, Mrs. T added, "*Immediately* after the last class, Mr. Coop."

So yeah, I trooped along to Mrs. Treneger's office *immediately* after the last class of the day. She pointed to one of her Alcatraz chairs and I sat, after first checking to see that the thing hadn't grown metal teeth since it last tortured me.

We stared at each other in companionable silence for a bit, at least it was companionable on my part. I don't think anyone could be sure what Mrs. T was thinking.

She was wearing a black dress with yellow trim on the neck and sleeves, which only made her more crow-like to my imagination.

"Now then, Mr. Coop," she finally said. "I understand you were kidnapped." She pursed her lips, tapped them twice with her fingertip, then unpursed them to add, "Tell me about it."

So I did. Turns out Mrs. T is a pretty good listener. At least that's what I deduced from the expressions on her face as I told the story. Her face shifted so nimbly from concern to astonishment to delight that I started to feel like I was narrating the latest audiobook thriller for her.

When I finished with Grogan and his cohorts being carted off to jail by the police, Mrs. T leaned forward as far as she could to cut the distance between us across her desk. She did that thing where she fixes me with one eye and then the other. Then she cleared her throat and said, "Now Mr. Coop, I guess that was quite the adventure."

I smiled. "Yes ma'am, it sure was."

"And you protected Mr. Sweetwater. As I asked you to do."

"Yes ma'am," I said again, still smiling.

She took a deep breath and let it out with a not-quite-silent whoosh. She straightened up in her chair and said, "Here's the thing, Mr. Coop. When I tasked you with protecting Mr. Sweetwater, I was imagining bullies, not armed thugs."

She raised her chin slightly and tilted her head to give me the one-eyed inspection. She held it long enough that I could see she was really worried.

"George Banner trying to steal his ham and cheese

sandwich," she continued. "Not this Grogan person and his criminal cronies pointing guns everywhere."

She put both hands flat on the desk, which I took as a sign that what came next was important.

"You mustn't put yourself in such danger, Mr. Coop. You could have been killed."

"I'll try not to Mrs. T," I said in my number one earnest voice, the one I reserve for parents, police and principals when I'm trying to convince them I'm going to do something I'm probably not going to do.

"You have a cell phone, use it to call the police," she said, apparently seeing right through the faux earnestness of my best earnest voice.

Grogan had kept us from using our phones to do exactly that, but I knew she meant that I'd have to see these things coming quicker and call the police before the situation got out of hand. I had to admit this was definitely good advice.

I looked her right in the eye and said, "Yes ma'am. I'll do that next time."

She held our eye contact until she was satisfied that I meant it, then she said, "Thank you, Mr. Coop."

She leaned back in her chair and dismissed me with a little wave of her fingertips. As I got to my feet, she smiled – yes, actually smiled – and said, "Well done, Mr. Coop."

# Chapter Sixteen

**As I was** leaving the principal's office, I got a text from my mom asking me to bring Augie with me when I came home from school. I suspected that she wanted to keep me closer to home after the Grogan escapade. On the plus side, a request like this usually meant baked goods of some sort. So when I pushed open the door to our small kitchen, I wasn't surprised by delicious smell of cookies. Orange peel oatmeal raisin, with walnuts – my favorite.

"Hi mom," I said, giving her a peck on the cheek while I tried to filch a cookie from the pile on the tray. She accepted the kiss but wasn't distracted from my real purpose in the least. She slapped my hand before I could lift one of the precious treats, and said, "Those are for my gardening club, but you can each have one later. After you talk to your father. He's in the living room."

Now that part of the deal was a surprise. Not the bad kind of surprise, because except for that one visit earlier, I didn't see him as often out here in the wilds of Anacortes. But still, he's a big city detective and I knew the job always threatened to snow him under. Days off were rare.

Augie and I passed cookie-less into the living room with my mom and found my father – what else – on the phone. As soon as he saw us, though, he said, "Gotta go" and immediately signed off and slipped the phone into his pocket. As he came across the room toward us, I saw that he was dressed differently than usual. Walking shoes, of course. How can you pound the pavement without the right shoes? Dockers khaki slacks, which were my dad's outdated idea of casually elegant. Short sleeved shirt, untucked. Now that was definitely a departure. This particular shirt had a gold badge embroidered on the left side of the chest, surrounded by the words *Seattle Police*. With a pleasant shock I realized it was one of Augie's bullet proof shirts.

My dad walked straight over to Augie with his hand out and said, "Thank you for these shirts, Augie. And for the custom embroidery."

Augie blushed as usual and said, "My pleasure, sir."

My dad gestured for us to sit on the couch while he took the facing chair.

"They arrived last Friday, enough for my entire missing persons unit."

Augie just smiled and nodded.

"Three for each of them. All the correct sizes."

More nods from Augie.

"No invoice," my dad said with a smile.

Augie smiled back and said, "My treat."

"Thank you," dad said. "From all of us."

My dad sat back in his chair and seemed to consider something. After a moment he said, "We tested them at the police range over the weekend. We put one on a pumpkin and did our best to fill it with holes." He held the tail of his shirt out. "Actually, this is the shirt we used." He smoothed the shirt back down over his belt and said, "As you can see, the shirt is undamaged. So was the pumpkin."

He put one hand on each knee, a gesture that I'd learned over the years meant that we were about to hear the heart of the matter.

"A young boy was found unconscious in the ferry terminal here in Anacortes early Saturday morning. Since the time he was found, the boy's condition has steadily deteriorated. He only came to my attention yesterday, after he had been transferred from Anacortes to the Medical Center in Seattle. We still don't know who he is or where he came from. To make matters worse, he's in a coma. The prognosis isn't good."

Dad blew a puff of air out of his cheeks, then wiped his mouth with the fingers of his left hand. That was also a sign I'd seen many times. It meant he was stymied by the situation and frustrated by his inability to resolve it. He leaned his elbows on his knees, bringing our little conservational group even closer.

"Coop, your mom has always given me good advice. In fact, I still call her when I'm stumped. When I told her about this mystery kid," he paused now and shifted his gaze to Augie, "she said to get Augie's help." My dad sat up, clapped his hands lightly together and put them back on his knees. Still looking at Augie, he said, "You impressed the hell out of me when you showed me your lab last week." He angled his head to look me over and added, "Coop's always impressed me. Few people his age can think on their feet like him. Always got his wits about him."

That was news to me, but it was nice to hear it.

My dad let those compliments sink in, then he said, "Here's the way I see it: this kid's story, at least my part of it, started in Anacortes. My son's living in Anacortes now and he's got a genius for a friend who has lived in Anacortes all his life. Maybe this is where I should start. I think your mom's right, Coop. Asking school kids for help might be crazy, but not asking them is even crazier."

Augie and I looked at each other, then we nodded together.

"Can we bring our friend Mika?" I asked. "We've sort of . . . well . . . it's like this . . ."

"We're a team," Augie said. "We need her with us on the case."

My dad looked over at my mom in surprise and I could see him mouth the words "the case?" to her. She gave him a look that I'm sure all my dads dreaded having aimed at them. It's a miraculous look, that in the space of an Augie-type nanosecond tells the lookee: "do it."

"Fine," my dad said. "Mika too."

"We're in dad," I said. "What do you want us to do?"

"Play hooky tomorrow."

"Skip school?" I said with a grin.

"Yep," my father said with an even bigger grin. "I'll set it up with your principal. I want you three to visit my young mystery man in the hospital."

# Chapter Seventeen

TUESDAY MORNING BART drove Augie, Mika and me down to Seattle again. When he stopped at my house to pick me up, I noticed a tiny green LED light above the rear tire. That meant Augie's solution to prevent another Grogan type kidnap had already been installed. I mentioned it to Bart, who smiled and said, "Yep."

Augie, after saying "Good morning," stuck his head in an iPad and stayed that way until we got to Seattle. I didn't mind – I was getting used to Augie's idiosyncrasies. Mika and I played chess – regular not double – and she cleaned my chess clock three games in a row. Bart brought us right to the parking lot of the medical center, where we met my dad and headed inside.

Things had already been set up with the hospital administration, so we went right up to the boy's room. My dad pulled the door open and walked in. Augie and I followed, me with some trepidation. Maybe you're thinking, Coop trepidatious? The guy as fast as a speeding bullet, the kid with fists like anvils? Yeah, I know. Hard to believe. But it got to me, all of it. The smells, the hushed halls, the anguish and heartache that slipped out from under the closed doors. I knew that people were hurting in this place.

Dad moved quietly to the foot of the single bed in the room. Augie walked over next to him and picked up the chart that hung on the bed frame, as confidently as if he had been one of the kid's doctors and was checking up on his patient. I hung back a bit with Mika, my lips pressed together and my hands slack at my sides.

The kid was on his back with a single white sheet pulled up to his chest. His arms were flat on the bed. Three plastic bags, each I supposed with a different kind of medicine, were hung from a pole by the bed, slowly transferring their contents into his arm by way of tubes connected to a needle in crook of his right elbow. His eyes were shut, long black lashes lying against his cheeks. The hair that fell across his forehead was dense and very dark, making me think the kid might be Asian. Chinese? Korean? Philippine? I confess that I am woefully ignorant of the physical differences in these races. But you've gotta ask yourself, why should it matter at all? People are people. We are all different, yet we are all the same. That's what makes living on this planet a kick in the ass.

Mika leaned close to the boy and studied his face. After a moment she straightened up and stepped back to stand with me. My dad looked at her, a question on his face.

"I believe he is Chinese," Mika said.

"You can tell that from looking at his face?" my dad said.

Mika nodded.

"From the shape of his eyes, the tilt of his ears, and the shape of his cheekbones."

"You're positive?"

Mika pursed her lips and glanced down before she looked up again and said, "No, of course not. He could be Korean or even Japanese, but I think he is most likely Chinese."

"What makes you an expert on racial characteristics?" my dad asked. It might have been a harsh question, but he asked it softly, with a sincerity that showed he was curious not sarcastic.

"I'm a Lummi Indian, Detective Cooperlick. As a Native American I can tell you that we tend to be more in tune to these things than some people."

"Than some white people, you mean," my dad said. He quickly raised a hand, palm up and added, "I know, that's me talking, not you. It's unfortunate, but true. Too many folks divide the world into white people on one side and everyone else on the other."

The room was silent after that, except for a faint rhythmic click and whooshing noise. Looking around, I realized it came from a clear plastic pump attached to a clear plastic tube that snaked down the kid's throat. Watching his chest rise and fall in concert with the machine, I could see that the contraption was breathing for him.

A rainbow of wires dropped from a computer monitor over the bed, each color attached to an electrode taped to different parts of his body. The signals sent back from the electrodes were displayed on the monitor, showing his heartbeat, respiration and a probably a bunch of other stuff the doctors and nurses needed to know. I just watched him tiptoe on the edge of life with his eyes closed and hoped that he made it back to safety.

Augie finished with the doctor's chart, then looked up at my dad.

"You don't know what happened to him?" he asked.

My dad shook his head. "No. He was discovered on the floor in the lady's room at the ferry terminal in Anacortes early last Saturday morning." My dad made a flat motion with his hand and added, "Unconscious. He hasn't regained consciousness since then."

Augie nodded slightly but didn't say anything. He just kept looking at my dad.

My dad, who still didn't quite know how to deal with an eleven-year-old boy who acted like a boss who was clearly expecting further information from his underling, blinked a couple of times and quickly made the necessary mental adjustment. He needed help and he didn't mind where it came from, so he continued his briefing.

"No ID. Simple clothes, all made in Hong Kong. He wasn't there when the facility was cleaned for the last time at two o'clock in the morning and he was discovered at five thirty that morning. So, we have a three-and-a-half-hour window when he could have gone in or been put there. We have no way of knowing whether he made it there under his own power or not." My dad held up his index finger to show that he had more, then he said, "There were some traces of sea water on the floor near the boy. Not unusual, given that the ferry terminal is next to the sea, but not common either. You fellas know how often it rains around here. People normally drip rainwater on the terminal floors, not seawater."

Augie nodded, then hooked the chart back on the bed-frame. He moved around to the side of the bed and gently lifted the sheet so that he could see the boy's chest and abdomen. He rearranged the sheet then did his thinking taps. That's what I called it anyway. It was a peculiar thing I'd noticed that he did when he was thinking. Or, given his stratospheric IQ, perhaps I should say when he was processing data. Anyway, what he did was put his right thumb under his right ear and lightly drum the other four fingers against his temple. He did that twice, then apparently the super-computer that was his brain had finished its calculations and all the available data had been analyzed.

Augie lowered his hand and asked my dad, "Did he by any chance have a bloody nose? Or perhaps a bit of blood in one or both ears?"

"Why yes," my dad said. "His nose and his left ear. Did you read that in the chart?"

"Oh, goodness no," Augie said. "I surmised that might be the case, because I suspect that your mystery child has been involved in a diving accident."

"A diving accident!"

That was Mika, not my dad. I think I was just as surprised as she was, but she got it out before me. My dad was probably surprised too, but he was better at controlling himself than either of us. He kept his attention on Augie and calmly asked, "Why do you think he had a diving accident?"

Augie regarded my dad quietly. I was afraid the next words out of his mouth were going to be, "Elementary, my dear Watson," but there was no levity in his tone when he said, "Five things. First, he was found near the sea. Second, the blood coming from his nose and ear indicate, among other possibilities of course, rupture of the nose and ear sinuses. Third, the skin over his ribs has a reddish splotch – by his elbow on the left side – that has mistakenly been recorded on his chart as a birth mark. Quite understandable in light of the similarly colored port wine birth mark that is plainly visible on his forehead. However, the marks by his ribs are a mild form of decompression sickness called *skin bends*. Fourth, there are scratch marks at the base of his neck and on his elbows. I believe he was experiencing a great deal of itching before he fell into this coma. The itching was most likely due to the dive injury that he sustained."

Augie paused there and my dad prompted him by saying, "That's impressive Augie, but you mentioned five reasons?"

Augie shrugged his thin shoulders and waved a hand over the whole rig: the kid, the bed and all the hospital machinery that was winking, blinking and pumping.

"Number five is the fact that he's in a coma."

My dad and I looked at each other, pretty much stunned by Augie's persuasive rundown. He wasn't finished, though.

"Of course," Augie said as he reached for the nurse's call button clipped to the pillow, "he's lucky that he's not paralyzed. He should be treated at the nearest hyperbaric facility without delay."

Things pretty much flew out of our hands at that point, but I'm happy to report that the kid is now in a recompression chamber and is being treated by a dive accident specialist. He's not going to be paralyzed, but they still don't know when – or if – he'll come out of the coma.

## Chapter Eighteen

**THERE IS AN** amazing chair in Augie's house. It's up on the second floor, facing a large window at the back. The view out that window? The blue-green waters of Fidalgo Bay. If you haven't seen it yourself, I'll tell you it's stellar, no matter what the weather. OK, there is a small matter of an oil refinery in the distance with a bunch of tanks and pipes, but still – it's a killer view.

The chair is a family heirloom, from his mother's side of course. I suspect any chair from Augie's father's side is likely to be an electric chair. Bart told me this particular chair was purchased by Augie's great grandfather on a trip to Norway around 1870. No one knows exactly how old it is, but the chair was already in an antique store back then, so I figure it's pretty darn old.

This chair is big, really oversized. It's mostly wood, but it has a worn padded seat made of red velvet. The back is nicely curved for comfort, which is remarkable since it was apparently carved out of a single slab of oak. I say carved because some really talented sculptor carved a lion's head into the wood. The lion looks right out at you and the detail is amazing.

So you'd think this chair would be the place to go with a cup of hot chocolate and a good book, right? Nope. This is where Augie goes to think. And when I say think, I mean just think. He sits there, scootched way back in the seat with his heels braced on the velvet pad. He's always looking down, with his head in his hands and his elbows braced on his thighs. That gorgeous chair might as well be in a closet, or directly in front of a brick wall.

On the Saturday after our visit to the kid in the Seattle hospital, Bart called me to ask for my help. He said Augie had planted himself in that chair like he planned to spend the rest of his life sitting there. Bart offered one of his sandwich specials – grilled peanut butter and jelly – to entice me over, although that wasn't at all necessary. I've gotta say, though, it's an outstanding treat, just don't let the hot jelly drip out. Anyway, when I finally climbed the stairs, I found Augie still in the chair.

"Augie, I hate to interrupt, but I was wondering," I said.

Augie didn't respond, although I thought he might have blinked.

"See the thing is," I said, "I bit my tongue while I was eating a grilled PB&J that Bart gave me."

Not even a twitch.

"So that made me think, wouldn't it hurt like crazy if a shark bit its own tongue?"

Nothing.

"You've got to loosen up a bit, Augie," I said.

Without lifting his head, Augie said, "Sharks do not have tongues."

"Lip, then," I said. "What if the shark bit his own lip?"

Augie's head finally came up and he said, "Sharks do not have lips either." He saw my grin and said, "Coop, you're having me on."

"I know you've got stuff to think about that I'll never understand . . . but Augie, maybe you're spending too much time in your own head." I pointed out the window. "Enjoy the view. Smile. Maybe even laugh out loud."

"Shark lips are worth laughing about?"

"Well yeah, if you're a teenager. Some things about being a teen suck and since you're almost a teenager yourself, you should know about them. Stuff like zits, hormones and parental locks on your computer. And sometimes *everything* sucks when you're a teenager without a driver's license. But . . ."

"But?" Augie said.

I grinned at him and said, "On the bright side, people expect you to be slightly demented once you hit the teens, so us teenagers can laugh our asses off at anything. The more absurd it is and the harder we laugh, the better."

Augie shook his head. "You might wish for my understanding of mathematics, Coop. But I shall always wish for your sense of humor. Sometimes I feel left out in the cold when I'm around other people."

"No sweat, Augie," I said. "If you aren't already laughing, I'll give you a nudge when something's funny. Mika will too."

Augie laughed at that, which was a good start.

"So Aug, what have you been thinking about all morning? You've been going at it so hard Bart was afraid you might strip a gear or blow a piston or something."

Augie closed his eyes and nodded. When he opened them, I could see that whatever he had been chasing in his head was still bothering him.

"I was thinking about that kid in the hospital," Augie said. "And about the orca that smashed the paddles of that Lummi canoe."

"Mmm, yeah. I see the connection," I said.

"You do?" Augie said.

I reached over and tapped his shoulder.

"That was your first funny nudge," I said. "You were supposed to laugh when I said that I see the connection, because that was a joke. No way, no how, could I make that connection."

"Ha ha," Augie said, rolling his eyes. "Now I get it. But listen Coop, some strange things have been happening. Well, not so strange if you consider them one at a time. And I think they may all be tied together. If that's true, then something very bad is going on, right here in Anacortes."

"OK, lemme see," I said. "We've got the Lummi guys getting their wrists busted by a killer whale. That counts as strange all by itself. The poor kid in a coma, well yeah, something's going on there, but finding out what's up with stuff like that is what my dad does. What else?"

"Why would an orca attack the Lummi paddlers like that?" Augie said. He sat up straighter and said, "What would possess an orca to use its dorsal fin like a weapon?"

"Orcas don't think that way?" I said.

Augie slapped both palms down on the armrests of his chair.

"Exactly! Humans think that way. Orcas do not think that way – unless they have been taught to think that way. Instructed to think that way."

Augie stopped talking and sat quietly. He raised his chin slightly, encouraging me to think through what he'd just implied. I took him up on the challenge. I brainstormed the things Augie had just said, turning them this way and that in my head: humans, orcas, thinking, taught, instructed, weapon, attack. Suddenly, I had it.

"Dr. Underwood," I said. "You said Dr. Underwood wanted you to make a brain coupler that would let you control another person. An orca's not a person, but then neither is Leo. You think Dr. Underwood is controlling that orca."

Augie's face split into a wide smile.

"Very good, Coop," he said. "Yes, I believe that someone has interfered with that orca's brain. I think it's been . . . well, reprogramed. Only not by Dr. Underwood. He's just a greedy scientist with no integrity. Underwood probably modified my original design and sold it to someone else or some other group."

"Who?"

Augie shrugged. "I don't know," he said, "but I have one other clue that may be part of this puzzle."

He stopped again, so I prompted.

"The clue, Augie?" I said.

Augie said, "Well, remember I told your father about my online chess partner named Shizuko? She's been living on Kowloon Island for the last six months. Her family was from mainland China, but they have been staying with relatives who own a large apartment in West Kowloon."

"West Kowloon?"

Augie nodded, but he looked troubled and I thought I knew why.

"You've been planning to meet your chess friend in person?"

"That's why Shizuko is part of what's bothering me, Coop," Augie said. "She told me last July that she would be coming to the United States, in fact to Seattle. We had planned to get together as soon as her family was settled in."

Augie turned toward me, the expression on his face going from merely troubled to downright anxious.

"But you still haven't heard from her?"

"Nothing. It's like she disappeared."

"OK, that's a problem. But why is . . . um . . . Shizuko, was it . . . possibly part of *this* problem?"

"I didn't realize it until I looked at a map earlier this morning," Augie said, "but Kowloon Island is part of Hong Kong."

He looked at me expectantly after he said that, so I thought hard for a moment.

"Oh, wait just a minute," I finally said, snapping my fingers. "The kid in the hospital – his clothes were from Hong Kong."

"Exactly!" Augie said.

He jumped to his feet and paced back and forth, overcome with nervous energy now.

"Shizuko didn't tell me much about how they were going to travel from Hong Kong to this country, but she did mention that they planned to spend a few days in Victoria."

"Which is less than four hours from here by boat," I said. I knew this because Kevin took my mom and me over there one weekend in his boat.

"Yes, that's right," Augie said. "And there's a ferry from Sidney, British Columbia, which is very close to Victoria, that makes regular trips to . . ."

"Anacortes," I supplied. "Where the kid in the Hong Kong clothes was found soaking wet and unconscious."

I got to my feet now – what is it about getting up and walking around that makes you think more clearly – and joined Augie in marching up and down. I agreed with him that something was going on, but so far it was impossible to say what.

"That's pretty sketchy," I said. "Maybe your friend's just too busy. Maybe lots of people come to the US from Hong Kong by way of Canada. Maybe . . ."

Augie stopped me with a raised hand, like a traffic cop.

"There's something you don't know Coop, that changes everything. I knew it, but I didn't know what it meant until this morning when I sat in my chair and worked it out."

"Worked what out?"

Augie walked over to the window and looked out over Fidalgo Bay. I don't think he was seeing the water, or even the oil tanks in the distance. He was looking intently around in his own head.

"Leo told me about a scary whale," Augie said.

He came out of his internal reverie and turned his head away from the window to look at me.

"You know what I mean when I use the word *said*,"

Augie said. "I mean Leo sent a thought to me and using sign language I refined what he meant until it seemed like we were having a conversation."

I nodded. Leo's thoughts were not that clear to me – more like flashes of images – but I didn't have Augie's experience with the brain coupler. Or the added advantage of using sign language with Leo.

"At the time, I assumed Leo's reference to a *whale* was to a *killer whale*. Like the orca that attacked the Lummi paddlers."

"That wasn't what Leo meant?" I said.

Augie shook his head.

"No. I don't think a dolphin like Leo would refer to an orca as a whale. In spite of commonly being called killer whales, orcas are actually the largest members of the dolphin family. When we talk about whales, we generally mean much larger animals, like humpback whales or bow-head whales."

"So you think Leo's scary whale was a humpback?" I said. "Or maybe some other big whale?"

Augie shook his head again.

"No, Coop, I don't," he said, "and here's why: whales are not scary to dolphins. Why should they be? Except for sperm whales, like the famous white whale from the novel *Moby Dick*, whales don't even have teeth. They have structures in their mouths called baleen, which they use to comb huge amounts of tiny shrimp-like creatures called krill out of the seawater. No Coop, dolphins and the large whales get along just fine. In fact, Leo told me that some of the whale songs are about dolphins."

"Really?" I said. "I know that whales sing and that the

sound carries through the ocean for hundreds of miles, but I didn't know they sang about dolphins."

"Apparently they do," Augie said. "Whale researchers think the whale songs tell the history of whales, a way to teach their children about what has happened in the past. But my point is that whales and dolphins have a friendly coexistence. There is no reason for Leo to describe a real whale as scary."

"A real whale?" I said. "As opposed to what?"

Augie looked back out the window before he answered. He took a deep breath and let it out.

"I think Leo was talking about a submarine."

"A submarine!" I said.

Augie didn't say anything else, he just let me connect the dots.

"Except for the whole Jonah fairytale," I said, "the main difference between whales and submarines is that submarines have people inside them."

"Exactly!" Augie said, stabbing a finger at me.

"We need to get my dad, my detective dad, out here," I said.

# Chapter Nineteen

It was Sunday afternoon by the time my dad could get away from his regular case load in Seattle. We met in the living room at Augie's house. Augie, Mika and I were the attendees, with Bart an interested onlooker. Augie had given my dad a summary of his thoughts, which resulted in my dad leaning close to Augie and assuming his official Detective Cooperlick voice.

"Let me get this straight," he said. "You're saying that the boy in the hospital, the one in a coma who can't speak for himself, was trying to sneak into the United States from Canada by submarine?"

Augie's not the kind of eleven-year-old kid to be intimidated by a burly police detective. He held his ground and nodded.

The burly police detective was likewise not one to be intimidated by an eleven-year-old, Einstein or not.

"And the sub had a malfunction?" he asked. "But the boy escaped?" He piled a generous amount of skepticism onto the words *malfunction* and *escaped*.

Augie calmly said, "Yes, that's correct."

Detective Cooperlick drew himself back and sat up straight. He sighed heavily and said, "I'm afraid you might be right, for three reasons." My dad held up a thick index finger and said, "The first reason is geography. It's a short trip through the San Juan Islands from Canada to the United States. Hundreds of small boats do it every day in the summer. You could easily make it undetected in a sub." He raised another finger and continued, "Second, shipping containers have been the favorite way for smugglers to get their goods into this country for many years. We have three big ports in the Pacific Northwest, including Seattle, Tacoma and Portland. Seattle alone handles well over a million shipping containers every year. But we have become very good at inspecting them. Special scanners, enormous x-ray machines and sophisticated tracking systems have made it difficult for the smugglers."

"So they go to Canada, instead," Augie said.

My dad nodded quickly.

"Very good," he said. "They go to Canada. Not to say the Canadians aren't vigilant, they just don't have the volume, so they rely on older methods like visual searches and paper records. It's just not as efficient."

We were all quiet for a moment. If everyone else was like me, they were picturing huge ships with shipping containers stacked ten high from bow to stern being unloaded by cranes into ports already jammed with thousands of identical containers.

Augie broke the silence and said to my dad, "And the third reason is the boy's clothing, isn't it? It was made in Hong Kong. I suspect that you've already looked into that and have something more to tell us."

A small smile turned up the corners of my dad's mouth, then he said, "Impressive deduction. Yes, you are correct. I contacted the Hong Kong police, and asked them about missing children."

He rubbed his hands together, then rested them on the table and sighed again.

He said, "Eventually a detective named Josh Kwan called me back. He said they had a few missing children, but none who matched the description I'd given him and none by the name of Shizuko Li." My dad looked intently at me, then at Augie. "But he said our mystery child may be part of a larger problem."

"Larger?" Augie said.

My dad nodded. "The Hong Kong police are missing entire families."

"Entire families?" Mika said.

My dad looked at her, then at me. I think he realized for the first time that we really were a team. He wasn't going to get help from one without the others.

He nodded and said, "Mom, dad and the kids. So far not the extended family, like nieces and nephews, but Detective Kwan told me that the number of missing families has been growing over the last three months. He's worried, very worried."

"Why would whole families disappear from Hong Kong?" Augie asked.

"You know that Hong Kong is claimed by China? That it was leased from China by England for ninety-nine years back in 1898?"

"Yes, I remember from world history class. The lease ran out in 1997."

"Right. And now China officially controls Hong Kong, but Hong Kong doesn't want to be part of China. For some time after the lease ran out, China didn't force the issue of who controls Hong Kong and they both existed in a tenuous peace. But that changed recently. Now China is exerting its authority and people in Hong Kong are scared. Refugees from China have been moving through Hong Kong to escape for years. Now that avenue of escape is being shut down. People are desperate to escape. And when people are desperate, they will risk anything or pay anything to escape."

Augie, a couple of steps ahead of me as usual, said, "And there are always other people ready to take advantage of their desperation. Like my friend Shizuko and her family."

My dad pointed his thick index finger at Augie and nodded.

"Exactly," he said. "Detective Kwan suspects that a group of Hong Kong drug smugglers have recently switched from smuggling drugs into the US to smuggling people. He said that this gang frequently brings the father across first. Supposedly this is so that the father can find a place to live, even get a job, before the mother and children make the risky trip. Detective Kwan and I agree that the real reason is so the smugglers can demand more money before the family is reunited."

"Do you know anything about this gang of smugglers?" Mika asked. "How many in the gang? What their names are? Where they keep the sub? Where they got it in the first place? How long they've been operating? When they are going to make the next run . . ."

My dad held up both hands, palms out, to ward off the flow of questions from Mika. He let silence settle into the room, then he said, "I'll be perfectly honest with you. The answer to your questions, to all of them, is no." He rubbed his forehead with his fingertips and shook his head. "I wish I had answers to all your questions, but I don't."

Augie raised his hand as though he was volunteering in class.

"I believe I have a way to get some of those answers for you," he said.

## Chapter Twenty

**AT PRECISELY FOUR** o'clock Monday afternoon, my dad was waiting for Augie, Mika and me in front of the hospital in Seattle. He had been watching for us, and opened the back door when Bart glided the Mercedes to a stop. He frowned at first when Augie climbed out wearing his Australian Akubra cowboy hat, but he managed to smile as he greeted us.

"Shall we head right up?" he said. "Detective Kwan in Hong Kong intercepted a phone call after we talked yesterday. He said something is about to go down with this gang. He thinks they're about to move the next group of people into the US. We have to hurry."

We moved quickly into the lobby and headed for the elevator. A woman in a white lab coat was waiting and she put a hand up to stop us as we approached.

"Dr. Ridgeway?" dad asked.

She nodded, lips pursed tightly and clearly holding in a good deal of agitation.

Dad held up his credentials wallet, open with his identification card and gold detective's shield.

"I'm Detective Cooperlick. We spoke on the phone earlier?"

"Yes, we did. And I'm still concerned that what you propose may be harmful to my patient."

The elevator door opened with a *ding!* and my father held his hand out inviting her to join us.

"Maybe we could talk on the way up?" he said. "The time factor has become even more critical since I first spoke with you."

She looked doubtfully at me and Mika, then even more doubtfully at Augie, who tilted his head back and gave her a smile from beneath the brim of his Akubra hat. She sighed, then turned for the elevator, motioning with her finger for us to follow. As the doors closed, we stood like people tend to do in an elevator, spaced evenly and all facing front.

Still looking straight ahead, the doctor said, "This morning I objected strongly to the hospital administrator about this invasion of my patient, but he wouldn't listen. I feel it is definitely not in the patient's best interest. Perhaps you can convince me otherwise?"

My dad said, "Well . . . I assure you, there won't be any invasion. Dr. Sweetwater has perfected a device that allows us to . . . let's use the term *monitor* . . . a person's brainwaves with such precision that we can actually receive images from that person's thoughts."

Dr. Ridgeway turned to my dad now, one eyebrow raised so high that it looked like someone had drawn a question mark on her face.

"Seriously?"

My dad nodded solemnly and raised a hand with two fingers together.

"Scouts honor," he said.

Dr. Ridgeway scoffed, rolled her eyes and turned to the front again.

"Then why isn't Dr. Sweetwater here?" she asked. "Why send a detective and a gang of kids playing cowboy?"

Right then the elevator reached our floor and the doors slid open. Doctor Ridgeway stormed off first then spun on her heel to confront us. We stepped into the small space she left us in front of the elevator, squeezing together so the doors could close without catching any of us on the butt.

"I'm Dr. Sweetwater," Augie said, sweeping off his Akubra with his left hand and sticking his right out for a handshake. Mika and I both had to turn away to hide our smiles.

Dr. Ridgeway looked at Augie's proffered hand, then back up to my dad. I could see her silently mouth the word "seriously" again. My dad grinned and nodded. Dr. Ridgeway had the good grace to blush slightly over her gaffe.

"Pleased to meet you, doctor," she said, taking his hand. "Perhaps you would be so kind as to tell me more about your invention."

"I can do better than that," Augie said. "How about a demonstration? Perhaps there is someplace we could do that in private?"

Dr. Ridgeway regarded Augie silently for another few moments. Still skeptical I thought. But she took a deep breath and did her heel spinning thing, once more crooking a finger for us to follow.

We trooped down the hall together and assembled in

the empty room next to the comatose kid. Augie asked Dr. Ridgeway to sit in the single visitor's chair, which put her head about on a level with his.

"As Detective Cooperlick mentioned," Augie said, "my brain coupler allows the wearer to receive images from another brain. It won't allow me to read your thoughts, not in sentence form or even parts of sentences. I'll have to stand quite close to you for it to function." Augie edged closer, then said, "Any questions before we begin?"

Dr. Ridgeway leaned back a bit and nodded.

"Will I feel anything?"

Augie's turn to nod.

"Yes, but it's not painful I assure you. A small tickle, but it'll be somewhat strange. Others have described it as an itch on their soul."

"Oh," Dr. Ridgeway said with a bit of doubt resonating in that single syllable. "Well, can I control which images you see?"

Augie smiled and shook his head. "No, apparently not. My device receives your brainwaves unfiltered."

"Oh," she said again with even more doubt evident. She sighed audibly, then she said, "Well, what the heck. Let's do it. Get your brain coupler out and let's see what's inside my head."

All of us laughed at that and Augie said, "It's built into my hat. I'll just push a button hidden in the leather band and we'll start."

"You're kidding," she said. She looked around and saw that all of us were serious now. She shrugged her shoulders and said, "Fine, go ahead."

Augie pushed the button.

Dr. Ridgeway closed her eyes, no doubt attempting to censor her thoughts. Augie raised his chin and looked off into . . . well, I'm not sure where he was looking. Into her brain I suppose.

After about thirty seconds Dr. Ridgeway smiled, then raised her right hand and gently placed it on top of her head. She smoothed her hair back a couple of times, then lowered her hand back to her lap. Augie stepped away from Dr. Ridgeway and pushed the button to turn the coupler off. Dr. Ridgeway's eyes popped open.

"Extraordinary!" she said. "I don't think I know how to describe that experience. Not an itch, at least not for me. More like a soothing caress." She looked at Augie, who had taken off the Akubra and set it on the empty bed. "What did you see?"

"A dog," Augie said. "A golden retriever I believe, although I am somewhat confused because the dog was apparently here in the hospital."

Dr. Ridgeway's jaw dropped, and she quickly covered her mouth with both hands.

"My sister's dog!" she said through her fingers. She slowly dropped her hands and continued, "A beautiful golden retriever named Daisy. She's been trained as a comfort dog and makes frequent visits to this hospital. Everyone loves Daisy. She has the most amazing effect on the patients."

"Ah," Augie said, "that explains it." He cleared his throat and said, "I also received a clear image of Detective Cooperlick, along with what I think was a phone number. In any case . . ."

Dr. Ridgeway stood abruptly, a sudden blush rising

with her. I noticed my dad blush too, something I didn't think possible. He quickly pulled a business card out of his pocket and held it out to Dr. Ridgeway.

"You were probably going to ask for my card," he said. "In case you have more information for me later."

"Of course," she said, taking the card without making eye contact with him.

Mika nudged me and then stood on her tiptoes to whisper in my ear, "Don't you just love it when it's the grownups who are uncomfortable?"

Dr. Ridgeway led us next door, where we finally got down to business. The kid was still in a coma, but he looked better than the last time I'd seen him. He was breathing on his own for one thing. He was still hooked up to a monitor that displayed the workings of his heart and lungs, but the message of the zigzag lines seemed to be that everything was normal. For someone in a coma, anyway.

Augie held the Akubra out to my father and said, "You should do it yourself."

My dad took the hat with some hesitation, so Augie added, "The images you receive are subject to interpretation. Plus, you may be flooded with many images. You'll know better than I which of them are important."

Dad nodded and carefully positioned the Akubra on his head. He pulled the visitor's chair close to the bed and sat down with his notebook handy on his knee. Augie reached over and pushed the power button on the headband.

"OK, sir," he told my dad, "the power is on. Just lean close and relax your mind."

I moved over so that I could see what my dad wrote in his notebook. For the first minute he didn't write anything at all. He just sat with his eyes closed and his head nearly touching the kid's. If you peeked in the door about now, you'd think my dad was listening as the kid whispered in his ear. Which I guess wasn't far from the truth.

I found myself fidgeting impatiently but stopped as soon as my dad put his pen into action. He wrote slowly but steadily, nodding as though he wanted the kid to know that he understood. Here's what he wrote:

*Clothes in backpack*
*Leave home*
*Swallowed by whale*
*Hungry, thirsty*
*Shouts*
*Father!*
*Dark, cold, wet*

At this point Dr. Ridgeway, who had been alternating her attention between the life sign monitor and the boy himself, put a hand on my dad's shoulder and said, "Detective Cooperlick, you need to stop."

My father looked up and saw that the doctor was pointing at the monitor, where the patient's heart rate had suddenly risen. He backed slowly away from the bed, to break the connection as gently as possible. When he was about five feet away, my dad slowly removed Augie's Akubra and passed it back to him. Augie held it by the brim and pushed the power button on the headband to turn it off.

We all stood there in a silent tableau, waiting to see what happened to the boy in the coma. If any of us was hoping for something dramatic, like the boy waking up and telling us the whole story, we were disappointed. His pulse rate gradually slowed to normal, but that was it.

Dr. Ridgeway cleared her throat and said, "What's next, Detective Cooperlick?"

Detective Cooperlick, who I suspect would like to have asked her out to dinner next if the situation was different, said, "We contact the FBI. They've always got jurisdiction in a kidnapping."

## Chapter Twenty-one

THE NEXT DAY, Tuesday, my father arranged with the Anacortes School principal that Augie, Mika and I could leave early again. I suspect that wasn't difficult because when I went to her office to collect our permission slips, Mrs. T was clearly intrigued that we were somehow involved assisting the FBI. She held the slips out to me but kept a grip on them until I promised a complete report.

After lunch, when the other students were filing back to class, we piled into the back of Augie's Mercedes and Bart once more whisked us toward Seattle. We made one stop at the police headquarters to pick up dad, who joined Bart in the front of the car for the short ride to the FBI building.

The Seattle field office of the FBI was exactly as I expected. Shiny marble floors, bright lights, tall ceilings. Everything marked with the FBI logo and photos of every official in the chain of government bosses, starting with the local Special Agent in Charge and ending with the president. After a thorough frisk in the lobby, we were escorted up to the ninth floor and down a long, spotless corridor decorated with more glossy photos of unsmiling officials. Our escort led us into a small conference room filled by a wooden table and six chairs. The wall facing out was floor-to-ceiling glass, with a stunning view of downtown Seattle. Out beyond the Space Needle, I could see one of the green and white Washington state ferries coming in from Bainbridge Island or maybe Bremerton. I had to pull my eyes back into the room and concentrate on the purpose of our visit as we were introduced to Special Agent James Todd and Special Agent James Harrington. Of course, they immediately became the James Brothers in my head.

James T was about six feet tall and trim, with smooth pinkish skin and short blond hair cut in a flat-top, which is a style you normally see on someone wearing a uniform, not a three-piece suit. He stood his hair up in the front with some kind of hair goop. That got me checking his fingers and sure enough, his nails were immaculate and finished with a glossy polish.

James H was the shorter of the two, maybe five ten and I'm sure he would have tipped the scales at two twenty, minimum. I'd be willing to bet that he had a regular sit-down with his supervisor to talk about how his diet was coming along. Not so good apparently. James H was also the older of the two, at least if hair line recession was an indication. He was dressed in a suit as well, his whole outfit conservative down to the black wingtip shoes.

We did the usual nodding, hand-shaking-pleased-to-meet-you thing, the two agents politely giving Augie, Mika and me the same courtesy they showed my dad. We all sat down and dad gave them a twenty-minute summary of his findings. He had his notebook handy, but to my amazement he never once had to check his facts as he ran through the details in perfect chronology. When he stopped, there was silence in the room. The two agents looked at each other, then one of them spoke. The Harrington half of the James Brothers I think, but I'd already gotten them confused.

"Seriously?"

That kind of dampened the mood, as you might imagine, because his tone clearly conveyed disbelief with a thick coating of derision.

James T hurriedly took up the narrative, attempting to smooth over his partner's rudeness.

"What my partner means . . ." he said. He paused, then decided he couldn't tell us what his partner meant with any greater politeness. He blew out a lungful of air, making his lips flutter in frustration. Then he took a deep breath in and said, "Look, stand in our shoes for a minute. You come in with a story about talking dolphins, submarines smuggling refugees and reading the mind of a kid in a coma." He held his arms out, palms up and lifted his shoulders in a world class shrug. "What are we supposed to think?"

James H jumped in on cue, tag-teaming us to give his partner a break.

"We have your contact info," he said holding up my dad's business card. "We'll look into it." He saw my dad frown, which I know from firsthand experience can be a scary thing, so he quickly added, "You have to admit, it's a wild story, no? But we are always happy to work with the locals. We'll check with our people and get back to you."

We were shuffled back to the elevators with the same plastic politeness they had shown from the beginning. When the doors slid closed and the elevator was safely on the way back down, my dad said, in a voice credibly like James H's but an octave higher, "We're happy to work with the locals." Then he grinned at all of us and said in his normal voice, "Maybe they should print that on their business cards?"

That relieved the tension a bit, but I could tell that he was fuming inside. All of us were upset, and not just at the way we had been summarily dismissed. Clearly no action was going to be taken by the FBI.

Bart had the Mercedes waiting at the curb outside the building. He opened his mouth to give a cheery *how-did-it-go?* type of greeting but closed it as soon as he saw our faces. We rode to the police headquarters in silence, but my dad turned in his seat to talk to us before he got out.

"Don't worry," he said. "They're usually not that arrogant, but I've always found that we get little real cooperation from the FBI. They always do, or not do, what they want. I'm going to work with my counterpart in Hong Kong and try to develop more leads." He got out of the car, but leaned back in and said, "Thanks. I'll take it from here, but I want you all to know I never would have gotten this far without your help."

We didn't say much on the drive back to Anacortes, which took longer than usual because we were just in time to join several thousand commuters clogging up I-5 in both directions. I don't think Augie even noticed. He sat quietly, kind of looking off into space until Bart finally left the highway at Route 20 and headed west for Anacortes.

"The only way to find that submarine," Augie said. "is to do it ourselves." He paused to see our reaction to that pronouncement. Without hesitation, Mika and I nodded in agreement. Satisfied that he could count us in, Augie said, "After school tomorrow, both of you should come to my lab. We're building a dolphin suit."

# Chapter Twenty-two

**AFTER SCHOOL ON** Wednesday, Mika and I discovered that when Augie used the phrase "we're building a dolphin suit" he actually meant that "he's building a dolphin suit." To be fair, it was obvious that any uninvited input from Mika or me would just slow him down. He did actually need me to be there, though, because he had to take measurements.

"You're a certified scuba diver, aren't you Coop?" were the first words out of his mouth when we got to the lab.

"Yep," I said. "Kevin's a scuba diving instructor, and he took me through the course."

"Excellent. You'll be our operator," Augie said picking up some kind of laser measuring device. No old school metal tapes for Augie. He had me stand straight, arms out to the sides while he measured up, down and sideways. Mika pulled up a chair and watched. Somehow, I suspected she knew more than I did. She'd already figured out what Augie had in mind, while I was still in the dark. As usual. When Augie had said "dolphin suit," I pictured something like a scuba diver's neoprene suit. Why would he need an operator for that?

"Operator of what?" I said.

"This, of course," Augie said. He climbed into the fancy purple chair in front of his semi-circular computer and brought up an amazing image. A space suit for dolphins. That's the first thing that came to my mind, assuming dolphins would ever feel the need for interplanetary travel. I could see that the measurements Augie had just taken had been fed automatically into the design before he blanked the screen.

"I need a couple of days to perfect the design and make the suit," Augie said. "Come back first thing after breakfast on Saturday for a fitting. Shall we say eight o'clock?"

Mika and I nodded obediently and slipped out of the lab. We split up outside and went back to our homes. I don't know about Mika, but I didn't get much out of school during the next two days. Mrs. T checked with me to make sure everything was all right, but no one else even commented on Augie's absence. I guess it wasn't the first time our prodigal inventor had stayed in the lab rather than show up at school.

A thick white fog descended on us Friday night and on Saturday morning Cap Sante was hidden from view. The mist played tricks with sound; sometimes muting the clang of bells on the navigation buoys and cries of the seagulls and sometimes making it sound like you were right next to them. I arrived on my bike at the lab a few minutes early and waited for Mika, who materialized out of the fog like a ghost on her own bike and glided up next to me. She said her parents had dropped her off at the traffic circle at the top of the street on their way to Whitby Island on tribal business.

"Ready, Mr. Dolphin Suit Operator?" she asked.

"Very funny," I said, reaching a finger out to the door-bell. Before I pushed it, we heard a click and the door swung open. We marched in and saw Augie at the upper railing.

"Come right up," he said.

Once we were upstairs, we found Augie standing next to a tall work stand covered with a large blue sheet. He smiled at us, then whipped the sheet away with a theatrical flourish. The dolphin suit hung there, looking like an astronaut suit from one of those glitzy science fiction movies. You know the kind, right? Earth has been destroyed and a hearty band of colonists have been in suspended animation for twenty-nine years while their spaceship flies through the empty reaches of space to the only inhabitable planet in the Alpha 40 quadrant of the galaxy: Planet XR1000. A lovely, hauntingly earth-like world of blue oceans and white-peaked mountains where, of course, the first colonist out the door of the spacecraft in a suit like that will die a horrible death.

I hesitated, thinking the unlucky sucker in that movie would probably look a lot like me. Mika noticed and quietly eased around me. She reached out and touched the shimmering material that coated the suit.

"The first one on the planet didn't always die in those movies," she said.

Sometimes I'm amazed at how easily she gets into my head. And without wearing one of Augie's brain wave coupling thing-a-ma-jigs. Remind me never to let her near me when she's got one strapped to her head. I'd never have another secret from her in my entire life.

Augie was already rattling off the features of his clever

design, like switches built into the helmet so that you could work them with your chin. He was particularly proud of the HUD – the Heads Up Display – that displayed all the suit's vital information, like depth, speed and heading, out in front of the helmet. When Augie went to get a cloth to polish the clear helmet, I realized that Mika was still watching me quietly.

"Yeah, so I'm scared," I whispered. "Augie's an incredible inventor, but the fact is *that* suit is completely experimental and totally untested. I'm supposed to take it deep underwater, which when you think about it, is just as dangerous for humans as deep space. Anybody in their right mind would be scared, don't you think?"

Mika moved in close to me and laid her hand on my forearm.

"Yes," she said. "It's natural to be scared."

"Thanks," I said with a nod, "although knowing that doesn't help much."

"My grandfather told me that before you can be brave, first you must know fear," Mika said.

"Uh huh," I said. "Well, I got the first part down cold, so I'm halfway to a silver star for bravery."

Augie hurried back and wiped what appeared to be an imaginary spot off the pristine helmet. He looked over the rest of the suit but didn't find any further need for the cloth. He stuffed it into his pocket and turned to us.

He said, "When the idea for this invention first came to me, I called it a dolphin suit." He nodded and reached out a hand to pat the suit. "That's actually a good name, because when you are wearing it, you'll have to surface every ten minutes or so to breathe – just like a dolphin."

151

"Really?" I said. "You couldn't just use a scuba tank?"

Augie shook his head.

"Too bulky, for starters," he said. "But most importantly, this suit will maintain sea level pressure at all times, just like the lungs of dolphins. That way you don't have to worry about decompression sickness or embolisms."

"Sounds good to me," I said. "How fast will it go?"

Augie grinned.

"I think you'll like this part Coop. Wearing this suit, you'll actually be faster than a dolphin underwater."

"Outstanding!" I said. I've always been a fan of fast. "How'd you manage that?"

"Three ways," Augie said. "First, it uses virtual streamlining technology to dramatically reduce drag. Here, help me take the suit apart and I'll show you."

With Augie directing us, Mika and I detached the helmet and shoulders, which came off as one piece. We set that part of the suit down on a workbench, then Augie had us arrange it so that we could see up into it.

"I've built a projector into the helmet right here," he said, putting his finger on a small obtrusion fastened to the inside of the helmet. "Remember the hat I gave you to protect your head when you rescued Bart from Grogan's thugs? This device is like that, but much improved. It continuously arranges the water molecules in front of the suit into a bullet-shaped virtual fairing. The fairing will look like a clear, pointed dome about eighteen inches ahead of the suit, even though there's actually nothing there but water."

Mika and I looked at the tiny projector and shook our heads in amazement.

"What's the second thing that makes the suit so fast, Augie?" Mika said.

"Well, that would be the propulsion system itself," he said.

Augie set the helmet on a nearby work bench, then moved back to the suit and started pointing out the components of the propulsion system to us.

"Water is taken in here, through these slits at the shoulders," Augie said. "Then the water molecules are accelerated magnetically through these flexible tubes built into the body of the suit."

He ran his fingers down the length of the suit to the feet, ending up on his knees next to the bottom of the suit. Mika and I knelt down with him to get a good look.

"The water is then ejected out these ports at the feet," he said. "Sort of like a jet engine that uses water for fuel. Except that the water isn't damaged in any way by the process. Oh and unlike a jet engine, this propulsion system will be nearly silent. I expect that the only noise will be a very faint, low-pitched rumble underwater."

I said I couldn't wait to try it out, scared or not.

"And the third thing?" Mika asked as all three of us stood up again.

Augie said, "You actually discovered that already, Mika. When you touched the suit earlier, it shimmered slightly, right?"

Mika nodded.

"OK," Augie said, "go ahead and give a good poke this time."

She reached out a hand and jabbed her index finger solidly into the chest of the suit.

A rainbow of color radiated out like a pebble dropped into a pond, except that the rainbow didn't flow outward in a circle. Instead it flowed from front to back and only died out when it reached the feet.

Augie said, "I should point out that the material that makes up the outside of this suit is a super thick version of my armored cloth. So, it's stronger than steel. But what makes it shimmer is a coating of something I call *nano-denticles*."

"What's a nano-denticle?" I asked. "Or a plain, ordinary denticle for that matter?"

"I didn't invent denticles," Augie said. "They already exist in nature. Sharks have them, for instance. They're called dermal denticles. They overlap like scales, but actually look more like teeth. A shark's denticles fit together in a way that smooths the flow of water over their bodies, making them fast and silent as they swim. My nano-denticles have interlinked nano-robots that do the same thing, but much more efficiently. The nano-denticles don't simply smooth the water flow, they increase it slightly. You saw how they shimmer from front to back? That's the nano-denticles at work, allowing the suit to move more quickly through the water."

There was one other prominent feature of the suit that Augie hadn't explained yet: a large shark-like dorsal fin.

"It's for stability," he said. "It'll help you go in a straight line and keep you from rolling over and over."

That sounded like an excellent idea, but I really liked two other things about the dolphin suit's dorsal fin. The first was that it was the same bright yellow as Leo's fluke. It might be silly, but it made me feel a bond of some kind with Leo. The second was that Augie had used a laser to etch a vegvisir on each side.

# Chapter Twenty-three

GETTING INTO THE dolphin suit turned out to be a bit complicated. You didn't just stick one arm in and then the other, like you were putting on a jacket. Augie had placed most of the electronic components in the helmet – engineering efficiency was the term he used. Made sense, I guess. You didn't want to have wires running everywhere if you could help it. That explained why the head and shoulders of the suit were constructed as one piece and the rest of the body was another piece. When the suit was taken apart, it looked like it had been decapitated. You fed yourself feet first into the hole where the head and shoulders would go, then the helmet part was slipped over your head and fastened to the lower half. Pretty slick, but getting me into the suit proved to be a challenge.

We finally laid the bottom part of the suit flat on the workbench, stomach down. I climbed up and wiggled into it. I could hardly move because the suit was so stiff and heavy, so we decided just to clamp on the top part while I was lying on the workbench. That worked fine and we discovered that the suit fit me properly and that all the controls worked the way they had been designed. Augie and Mika unclamped the top and bottom of the suit and helped me out.

"The next thing on my check list," Augie announced, "is a test ride."

I stood up, thinking it would be best to get it over with. Just in case I had second thoughts later. "Let's go now," I said.

"I'll get Bart to help us load it into the Mercedes," Augie said. "We can put the top into the trunk and the bottom in the passenger area. We'll have to scrunch ourselves in with it, but I think we can fit."

"I'll call Kevin," I said. "He's already agreed to take us out in the *Golly Gee*. He doesn't have a charter today, but he's down at the marina anyway."

"Wait!" Mika said.

When Augie and I turned to see what she wanted, Mika reached into her pocket and took out three small plastic packets.

"These arrived by UPS yesterday. I was going to pass these out later, but this seems like a good time."

She opened one of the packets and tilted something into her palm. It was a small bronze pendant, a vegvisir. It was attached to necklace fashioned from a slender leather thong. She reached up and draped it over my head. The vegvisir settled comfortably at the base of my neck. Mika touched it lightly, then stepped back to check it out.

"Perfect," she said.

It was probably just the bronze metal, but I swear I could still feel the warmth of her touch through the pendent as she put an identical one around Augie's neck. She had Augie hold his hands out and she tipped a third vegvisir out of the last packet. This one was gold instead of bronze; plated of course, Mika was quick to point out. Hers also had an elegant gold chain instead of a leather thong. Augie and I both held the chain open for her as Mika slid her head through.

We admired each other's, then Mika said, "Symbols like this are probably more important to me, being a Lummi Indian, than to either of you, but I'm glad you are wearing them."

I looked over at the dolphin suit, then back to Mika.

"Right at this moment," I said, "I'm in favor of all the help I can get." I stooped to grab one side of the helmet and shoulders portion of the suit. "Now, shall we get this thing loaded?"

We wrestled the top half out the door of the lab and over to the Mercedes, then Bart helped us with the rest of the transfer. By the time we arrived at the Cap Sante marina the tide was high, so the ramp leading to the floating docks wasn't steep, but a heavy fog was still choking the brightness out of the day. Kevin was down at the *Golly Gee*, checking the engines, the bilges, the radar and all the other things that he always checked before each trip. A tall, lean man with blue eyes and short blond hair bleached by long days in the sun, Kevin looked the part of a charter boat captain. He had the hatch covers up on both engines, but waved when he saw us and motioned for us to come on down.

With Bart's help, we loaded the suit into a couple of the marina's courtesy carts and wheeled them down to the boat. Kevin had the boat ready to go by then and he helped us stow the suit in the cockpit. When we were ready, Bart untied the lines and waved as Kevin backed the *Golly Gee* out of the slip.

Mika offered to help Kevin with the boat, so he brought her up to the fly bridge as we motored out of the Cap Sante Marina. He slowed down and put the boat in neutral, then started to give her a lesson on how the controls worked – the throttles, the shifters and the helm – but he stopped talking when she slid confidently into the captain's chair, dropped the port transmission into forward and the starboard transmission into reverse. She spun the boat smoothly around on its own axis, then slipped both transmissions into forward, timing the maneuver so that the boat chugged off exactly on its previous course.

"My Uncle Jake is a salmon fisherman," she said, glancing over at Kevin and smiling at his astonished look. "He allows me to drive his boat sometimes."

"Right," Kevin said, adjusting to Mika's unexpected prowess with a grin of his own. "Can you navigate, too?"

"*Red-Right-Returning* is the mnemonic my uncle taught me to help remember how the marker buoys work. We're outbound, so it's the opposite. Green buoys stay on the right side." Mika pointed at the buoy that was floating about a football field ahead of us. It was painted green and I could just make out the number "1" painted in white on the top. "I'll keep that green buoy on my right."

"Outstanding!" Kevin said. "Run the engines up to fifteen hundred rpm. That'll make our speed about five knots. We have to take it slow in the fog, right?" After saying that he flipped a switch on the VHF radio that would automatically sound a five second blast of our foghorn every two minutes.

Mika edged the throttles forward, settled on fifteen hundred rpm and turned her head slightly to listen to the sound of the exhaust. She eased the port throttle back until the even sound of the exhaust told her the engines were synchronized.

Kevin grinned. "Steer a course out Guemes Channel and then across Rosario Strait and into Thatcher Pass," he said. "We'll be going up the west side of Blakely Island." Mika gave him a thumbs up but kept her eyes on the water ahead as she motored by the number one buoy. Kevin nodded in approval and said, "I'll be back up after Coop and I get Augie's dolphin suit strapped down."

Down in the cockpit Kevin and I worked together to tie the suit down so that it wouldn't slide around as the boat moved. We arranged it on the floor of the cockpit and fastened a couple of lines to each side. We left plenty of room so that I could slide myself feet first into the suit when we were ready to start the test. It was fortunate that the *Golly Gee* had an extra wide transom door, which opened outward and could be pinned in place against the outside of the transom. That gave us a straight shot from the cockpit floor to the big dive platform. We checked to make sure the suit would fit through and then locked the transom door closed.

"Fancy piece of gear your friend invented," Kevin said, looking down into the helmet. "What's that button for?"

"Um, that's not a button. It's the video camera lens. The camera will record everything I see."

"Ah. Can we see it live?"

"No, sorry. Augie says we'd need a wire connecting to the suit in order to get a live feed from the video and that would limit us too much."

"Sure, of course. How about this lever thing?"

"That's for the exterior lights, Kevin. See here on top of each shoulder? That's not a lever, really. It's an on/off switch. I can push it with the side of my head to turn the lights on or off."

"OK, that's smart." He moved his light around the entire inside of the helmet and then he asked, "Where's the mouthpiece? Don't you have a regulator to supply air?"

"Umm, no Kevin. It's really like a dolphin that way. I hold my breath."

"What? So you can only stay under for a minute or two? How do you get another breath when you need it?"

"See this port here on the back of the suit? Just ahead of the dorsal fin?"

I put my finger on the port, which I couldn't blame Kevin for not noticing before. It was streamlined into the shell of the suit. He leaned down for a closer look, then said, "Got it. So you dump the stale air and take in fresh air using this port."

"Right," I said. "But I don't have to do it myself. A high speed, a high-volume pump does it for me, automatically. The instant the port senses that it's clear of the water, it blows the old air out this hole on the left side and sucks in fresh air on the right. It changes the air in the entire suit in less than a half second."

"Amazing," Kevin said. "But you've still got to hold your breath?"

"Yes, but there's always enough air in the suit for me to

hold my breath, exhale and take another breath five times. I can go about seven minutes before I have to skim up to the surface so the suit can renew the air."

"Wow. This suit really is like a dolphin."

I nodded. "And like a dolphin, I don't have to worry about the bends. The pressure in the suit is always at one atmosphere – just like up here on the surface. It stays that way no matter how deep I go. Plus, I can go up and down as fast as I want without giving myself an embolism."

Kevin looked at me skeptically. "Uh-huh," he said. "Tell me, how deep can you go in this contraption?"

I hesitated and Kevin picked up on it.

"You're not sure?"

"Not exactly," I said. "I mean, it's never been tested. But Augie says it's definitely good down to three hundred feet. He thinks it might be OK as deep as four hundred. Beyond that he's not sure."

"Not sure? You've looked at the charts with me many times, Coop. You know there are many places out here where the water's eight hundred feet deep. Or more."

"I know. But check this out." I reached inside the helmet and flipped a switch that was protected by a red metal flap. The suit powered up and I tilted the helmet so Kevin could look out through the front.

"I'll be damned . . . I mean danged. You've got a HUD."

"Cool, isn't it. A heads up display, just like the fighter jets. Once I'm underwater the display will show depth, the direction I'm heading, my speed and the distance back to the boat."

"OK Coop, I'm impressed. Listen, be careful down there, all right? I've got my scuba gear and a dry suit just in case I need to come and get you." He paused to make sure he had my full attention, then said, "But remember, one hundred and thirty feet is the sport diving limit. I'll push it down to two hundred feet if I have to, but you can go so far and so deep that I might not be able to help at all."

"I'll be careful," I said.

He slapped me on the shoulder and said, "I know you will Coop."

We both started for the ladder to the fly bridge, but he turned back and pointed at the base of the dorsal fin.

"I meant to ask," he said, "what's this symbol?"

"It's a vegvisir. From Norway in the olden times. It's kind of a compass, one that'll guide you when the going gets rough."

"Uh-huh," Kevin said again with about the same degree of skepticism as when he asked about the suit's maximum depth rating. He put an arm over my shoulder and pulled us toward the fly bridge. "Good move, putting that vegvisir doohickey on the suit. I've got a feeling you may need all the help you can get."

## Chapter Twenty-four

UNDER KEVIN'S WATCHFUL eye Mika steered us across Rosario Strait and into Thatcher Pass. The fog lifted as we approached Blakely Island, so we were able to turn off the fog signals. Dad told Mika to bring the engines up to 3,500 revolutions per minute, which she did by advancing the throttles in smooth increments. By the way he was nodding his head and smiling, I figured Kevin was thinking of offering Mika a job as his first mate.

"We'll drop anchor by this reef," he said, putting his finger on the chart next to a small lighted tower. "We'll have some nice deep water." He looked pointedly at me and added, "But not too deep. The visibility should be good and slack water will be in twenty minutes, so we'll have very little in the way of currents."

I leaned over to see where he was intending to anchor and saw with a surprise that the reef was named Leo Reef. Just a coincidence, but it made me feel good. The deepest water shown on the chart right near the reef was twenty-three fathoms. One fathom equals six feet, so doing a quick multiplication and rounding off I figured I'd be looking at one hundred- and forty-feet max. That was perfect. I didn't intend to go deeper than a hundred feet, but if by some chance I ended up on the bottom, I could be rescued by Kevin wearing his scuba gear. Maybe.

While he and Mika ran the boat, Augie and I climbed back down the ladder to the cockpit. We knelt by the dolphin suit so that Augie could go through the operating procedure with me one more time. The big diesel engines were driving the boat at cruise speed and we had to speak loudly to hear each other over the noise. We were both mesmerized for a few moments though, because the vibration of the deck from the engines and propellers churning away right below us caused the nano-denticles in the skin of the dolphin suit to react. They shimmered up and down the length of the suit, as though it had a life of its own and was eager to get in the water. The suit was a semi-shiny silver color normally, but now it was transforming chameleon-like from silver to gold, orange to red, purple to blue, then back again. Over and over.

Augie put his hand on my shoulder, leaned close to my ear and said, "Go ahead and crawl in. I'll help you go through the checks."

I nodded and stood up. I stripped off my jacket revealing the get-up that Augie insisted I wear. It looked like I was wearing one-piece long underwear, kind of like a cowboy might have worn on a cold north Texas winter back in the old days. Except my outfit was thick, black and sleek, and didn't have a flap in the back so I could visit the outhouse without getting undressed. My suit was actually similar to the inner garment for a diver's dry suit, and it would keep me warm inside the dolphin suit even though the water temperature would only be forty-five degrees.

I fed myself feet-first into the suit, glad that Augie had lined it with more of his nanobot material. The suit was not very flexible – I could bend up and down a bit; left and right a bit – but it was extremely comfortable. My heels fitted into stirrups mounted in the bottom of the legs, and my toes fit into sleeves that actuated small, electrically driven controllers when I flexed them up or down. The left foot pushed the back of the suit from side-to-side and the right foot pushed it up and down.

I had to scrunch my shoulders together to get my arms inside the suit and then work my hands down each sleeve. There were grips located in the ends of each sleeve for my hands. The main purpose of the grips was to let me control the angle of the fins mounted on the end of each arm. Augie explained that the controls in the feet would work like the controls on the tail of an airplane. The fins on the arms would work like the ailerons on the wings. Since I didn't have a pilot's license and had never flown a plane, Augie had demonstrated with a model P-51 Mustang that he'd built from a solid block of aluminum when he was six years old. You know, like any other six-year-old playing around with his new computer-guided, three-dimensional, waterjet cutting machine. Anyway, I had gotten the gist of how the controls worked. Use the arms to turn and climb, use the legs so you don't just skid sideways. Flying underwater. Piece of cake, right?

Each grip also had a trigger-like switch that I could work with my index finger. The right side was a throttle, spring-loaded so that if I released it, the suit's thrust dropped immediately to zero. But . . . no brakes on this super suit. I could slow things down slightly with the hand fins, but I'd have to be careful not to run into stuff down there. That was one of the things Augie wanted me to work out during this test dive.

The left grip had another trigger switch and as far as I was concerned it was the most important feature of the suit. Holding that switch in let me be in mental contact with Leo. I still had to be close to Leo underwater, but Augie explained to me that water conducted the brain waves much more efficiently than air. He thought I should be able to establish contact with Leo from as far away as ten feet, which was good because when we go after that sub full of mothers and kids, I'll be depending on Leo to help me get them up safe. Heck, I'll be depending on Leo to keep me alive. Thinking about an angry killer whale that's twenty-five feet long, weighs five tons, has forty or fifty long, sharp teeth and wants nothing more than to chomp down on my butt made me kinda . . . well, let's just say anxious would be a wild understatement.

When I had my arms and legs in the suit, Augie flipped the power on. "Let's check each system. First, give me a short burst with the accelerator."

"OK," I said. I gave the trigger under my right index finger a quick tug. The suit immediately made a low humming noise and lurched forward slightly.

"Good, good," Augie said. "Of course, we're out of the water now, so the suit doesn't have any traction so to speak. You'll get a bigger reaction underwater. Next, try the foot controls. Side to side first."

I lifted my left toe up, then pushed it down. I could feel the suit rock back and forth, just slightly.

"Excellent," Augie said. "And I see you remember which foot does what. OK, up and down now."

I nodded, then performed the same action with my right foot. The suit rocked on the deck again, up and down this time.

"That's all the control checks," Augie said. "You may as well stay in there. As soon as we . . ." He stopped as we felt the engines come down to idle. Augie squatted down so that he could see my face and said, "We've arrived at Leo Reef. After Mika and Kevin get the anchor down, we'll button you up and launch."

Augie stood up and stepped back out of my range of vision. I figured he was going to see if Mika and Kevin needed his help. I took a deep breath and tried to relax. I also tried not to think about being *launched*. It sounded too much like a torpedo. I'd seen a re-run of the classic submarine versus destroyer movie, *The Enemy Below* and that sort of dialogue was still rattling around in my brain.

*Captain: Fire one!*

*Crewman: One's away. Running straight, hot and true.*

*Captain: Time to impact?*

*Crewman: Forty-five seconds.*

Believe me, the word *impact* shouldn't be rattling around in your head when you're about to be launched.

# Chapter Twenty-five

AS WE HAD approached the spot Kevin and Augie had picked for the test ride with the dolphin suit, Kevin had asked a question I'd been meaning to ask myself.

"I've been watching and I haven't seen Leo following the boat," he said. "How does he know where to meet us? I mean, saying something like 'meet us at Reid Harbor' wouldn't mean anything to him, would it? Reid Harbor is what we call the enclosed bay at Stuart Island, but dolphins must have their own name it."

"Absolutely correct," Augie said. "When we were teaching Leo to understand sign language, we also showed him photos of many prominent land marks and what we call them. Like the Turn Point Lighthouse on Stuart Island, for instance. Very distinctive."

"Oh, sure," Kevin said. "That makes sense. Dolphins look around above the surface of the water all the time." He thought for another moment and then asked, "Did Leo tell you what name dolphins use for the Turn Point Light?"

Augie and Mika simultaneously burst out laughing.

"Oh yes," Mika said. "The dolphin name for that lighthouse is a long and completely unpronounceable series of click and squeals. Leo generously agreed to learn our names rather than make us learn his."

"Tell him the Leo Reef story," Augie said with a grin.

Mika matched Augie's grin and pointed to the chart.

"We're headed here, right? Leo Reef? Well Leo knows his nickname is Leo and when we told him there was a reef called Leo Reef, he was confused at first and then astounded. He said, 'You named it after me?'"

Augie said, "We didn't have the heart to tell him otherwise."

Leo was waiting for us at his reef, which made me wonder if he hangs around there now. Why not, if it's named after him? Anyway, I got suited up and the rest of them launched me. The first part of the test ride went fine. The suit was so cool. Everything worked exactly as Augie had said and I was having a great time. Ten minutes into the test ride, the throttle stuck wide open!

The HUD showed my speed at twenty-three knots. If you don't think that's fast, consider this: killer whales have been clocked at twenty-four knots, but only for a few seconds. Or this: at this speed I would cross the channel between Leo Reef and Blakely Island in less than three minutes. And this: the side of Blakely Island is so steep that it's essentially a granite wall.

I zigzagged like crazy, all the while trying to get my finger under the speed trigger and un-wedge it. Leo stayed with me for a minute or so, but he couldn't keep up for long and dropped back. I glanced at the HUD and was terrified to see that my speed was now twenty-eight knots. Nuclear attack submarines can go this fast underwater, but only a certifiably insane captain would run so fast in a narrow channel. When the HUD display clicked up to thirty knots, I decided my only hope was to fly.

Yep, Yardley H. Cooperlick was gonna be the first – and most likely the only – person ever to breach in a dolphin suit.

I pulled around in the tightest turn I could manage, until I was pointed in the general direction of the boat. I scanned the HUD quickly: ninety-two feet deep, heading northwest, one hundred and fifty meters from the boat and – yikes! – speed now thirty-two knots. I kicked my heels up to rotate vertically, steered up with the hand fins and zoomed for the surface. I passed seventy feet deep going straight up. I was relieved to see that I'd bled off some speed, not that two knots make a lot of difference when you're doing thirty. At fifty feet a shadowy figure suddenly appeared right next to me. My heart nearly stopped before I realized it was Leo, hammering through the water for all he was worth, trying stay up with me for a couple of seconds. When he was close enough for thought contact, he shoved one loud, hard image into my brain: *BOAT!*

I looked up to see the boat's huge dark shadow directly above me. I pulled back desperately on the hand fins.

Thirty feet – still on a collision course.

Twenty feet – why was that boat so big?

Ten feet – maybe, just maybe.

Five feet – oh man, it was gonna be so close.

I shot out of the water.

Augie, Mika and Kevin had all been leaning over the side of the boat looking down and I nearly took their heads off. I left the surface of the water leaning backward just a fraction. Mika's face couldn't have been more than two feet from mine when I rocketed past her. I hoped the suit's camera was able to preserve her look of complete astonishment for all eternity, but I know I'll keep it fresh in my memory anyway.

I must have risen at least twenty feet in the air. At the top of my arc, I rotated slowly onto my back. Not because of anything I accomplished with the controls of the runaway suit; my flight path was pure physics. Nothing but momentum, gravity, weight distribution and a bit of drag. Augie probably understood the dynamics of the whole thing in real time. I hope he enjoyed it. To me, it seemed to happen in slow motion. I just rode the suit down and can only describe my re-entry into the ocean as a monumental reverse belly flop.

I'm sure the splash was epic, but all I cared about was that the impact freed the throttle. The lever was finally kicked loose, and the suit stopped. Before I could sink, Kevin maneuvered the boat over, and Mika managed to get a boat hook under one of my arm fins. Together they dragged me unceremoniously up onto the dive platform and into the boat. One last push from below told me Leo had helped as well.

## Chapter Twenty-six

**PIZZA. THAT'S WHAT** I craved after the *Great Runaway Dolphin Suit Escapade and Aerial Display*. We ordered takeout from Anthony's Piece-a-Pizza-Pie and adjourned to Augie's house, minus Kevin who had a last minute charter.

We had wanted to conduct the test of the suit in secrecy and by luck we had succeeded in spite of my out-of-the-water antics. But after watching the video for the third time as we devoured a large pizza, I thought we should have sold tickets. It was *so* cool.

Mika had had the presence of mind to video the top-side part of the test with her smart phone, in beautiful high definition. She quickly edited the whole event into one movie, starting with footage taken from the flybridge as I slipped feet first into the suit. She alternated between the footage from her phone and from the camera inside the suit. It was neat to see the suit enter the water from both my perspective inside the suit and theirs on the deck. Leo starred in the underwater portions, until the throttle jammed full open. I was fascinated by how fast Leo could swim. His motion through the water looked effortless.

Even when he was going flat out to try and keep pace with the runaway suit, he was smooth as silk.

But the best part of the film by far was the breach. Mika switched between her outside camera shots and my inside camera, dropping into slow motion as I left the water. My hands came out first, or rather the suit's flippers with my hands controlling them. Then my head in the suit's clear helmet. In slow motion you could see water streaming off the virtual fairing that Augie's invention created just ahead of the helmet. Because of the virtual fairing, the helmet itself was dry as it burst out of the sea, so my head was clear behind the glass. The expression on my face was equal parts fear and exhilaration. A laughable combination if the loud guffaws of the others was the barometer. I thought I looked . . . well, adventurous.

After we watched the movie several times and Mika finally grew tired of saying "Ooh, look at the expression on your face Coop" as the helmet zoomed out of the water, Augie gave us a bit of bad news.

"The suit's range is more limited than I anticipated," he said. "And besides, even if we had unlimited range, we can't simply send Coop down to search here and there for the sub. We'd never find it."

"Good point, Aug," I said. "But what can we do about it?"

Augie did his patented *look-off-into-space* thing, which this time only lasted for about twenty seconds. But I'd guess that he probably completed ten million calculations during that short period. He seemed to arrive at a solution, because he gave an abrupt little nod then returned to earth.

"We need to talk to Leo," he said.

## Chapter Twenty-seven

**IN THE PACIFIC** Northwest people don't tan; they rust because it rains so much. But usually it's a light rain, maybe even just a sprinkle. Soothing, really. Not many of us even carry umbrellas, although we do love our waterproof, breathable Gore-Tex jackets. Today's rain was the kind of drumming rain that could dent concrete and drown unwary cats. And I was pedaling madly through it at five o'clock Sunday morning because Augie had called and said come right away.

I've never seen Augie wear a watch. Or even look at a clock for that matter. He lived according to some unique-to-Augie internal clock. I'm starting to imagine that if you could actually see Augie's internal clock, it wouldn't look like the ones that you see on walls everywhere. It would probably have two minute hands, two hour hands and run backwards with the numbers all jumbled up. If it was a digital clock, it might as well display random numbers. I'm not sure if it's because of his nightmares or simply because his incredible brain has a finicky on/off switch. All I know is that Augie doesn't sleep when the rest of the world sleeps.

This morning he said I had to come to the lab right away; he'd made another breakthrough.

I dumped my bike against the porch where Bart wouldn't back over it by accident and ran through the puddles to the lab. As soon as I approached the door, there was a quiet click I could barely hear over the rain, and it opened. I hurried inside, hung my dripping coat on a peg and called out to Augie.

"Up here," he said, looking over the railing on the second floor. He waved me up, so I ran up the stairs. I found Augie standing in front of one of his workbenches. He stepped aside so that I could see what he had been working on. I moved in close and looked the object over.

I have to say it wasn't particularly impressive. None of the color-changing nano-bots, no antennas, no wings, no wheels. It was smaller than my fist. About half the size, in fact, and it had a large hole in the center. There were some slots running vertically on the sides and these were covered by smooth grills of some sort. By now I was used to Augie's brilliant designs though, so I smothered my disappointment.

"Very nice," I said. "What does it do?"

Augie made a little chuffing noise in his throat. "*Obviously*," he said, "this is the artificial larynx I've been working on for the last two weeks. I've redesigned it to fit in the blowhole of a dolphin. It will let Leo talk."

# Chapter Twenty-eight

MIKA JOINED US for lunch; cheddar cheese and sliced apples on grilled sourdough bread, another of Bart's delicious sandwich specials. She was excited about the prospect of Leo actually speaking, but she brought up the question of whether or not Augie had the right to implant an artificial larynx into a dolphin. All of us knew, without having discussed it but also without any doubt, that Leo was a being equal to humans – equal at the very least. Performing a procedure like this on Leo had the same ethical requirements as performing one on another human. Unlike the emergency operation where Augie had repaired Leo's badly damaged fluke with Bart's assistance, this was not a necessary medical procedure. Without the patient's permission, it could not be done. Augie said he had explained the whole thing to Leo: what he would gain, what the risks were, how long it would take, the whole shebang. Leo had given his wholehearted permission. He was eager to have the operation.

As far as Augie was concerned, the operation was good to go. I had to ask another ethical type question, because

I knew Dad Four would be disappointed if I didn't. You see, my fourth father, Dr. Tim Raymond, was a veterinarian in Seattle. He would want to see Augie's qualifications. Namely, his license from the sovereign State of Washington to perform medical procedures on an animal. Augie, in spite of having a graduate degree that granted him the title *doctor*, did not have one that made him a veterinarian type doctor. And although Bart has proven himself to be exceptionally capable, he also lacked formal medical training. The obvious solution was to call Dr. Tim, so we did.

Fortunately, when we told him what we wanted to do, my Honorable Number Four Father came aboard in a flash. Sunday being a normal day off for him, he drove up to Anacortes through the rain that was still pelting down and spent nearly three hours examining the larynx, the lab and of course Leo. He was particularly fascinated with Augie's brain coupler and practiced with it for quite a while. In the end, he agreed to help. However, he said that Augie had a greater understanding of exactly how the device should be implanted, so Augie should perform the operation, while he assisted. He left as the rain finally tapered off but agreed to return as soon as we had a time scheduled for the procedure.

We still weren't ready to go. The only remaining difficulty was that Mika insisted that we get permission from Leo's mother before proceeding with the artificial larynx. My dad, I mean Dad One – the detective – had called me again late yesterday to say that his Hong Kong contact had new information that the next smuggling attempt from Canada was going to happen soon. They didn't have specific information, but one of their informants had heard that the sub was being readied at its secret base. Mika was adamant in spite of the urgency.

"We don't know how old Leo is," she said, "or even how old dolphins have to be before they're considered adults." She held her palms up and shrugged her shoulders. "What is the dolphin equivalent of eighteen? Or twenty-one? We can't just assume that Leo is capable of making a decision like this by himself."

Augie did his thinking pose, thumb and finger on his chin.

"I believe you're correct," he said with an emphatic nod. "We'll consult the mother."

After some discussions with Leo by means of sign language and the use of Augie's brain coupler, we set up a meet with his mom. Which was pretty interesting in itself, because of course dolphins don't wear watches or tell time the way we do. Setting up a meeting for say, 8:30 Thursday morning was totally meaningless to a bottlenose dolphin. We ended up using the tide and current predictions for Rosario Strait, the times of sunrise and sunset and the phase of the moon to nail down a time that all of us understood.

Unfortunately, the time we agreed upon was six o'clock Monday morning. Augie had gotten me up before five o'clock this morning and it was already after nine in the evening. Bart suggested that Augie hold a sleepover, which was a great idea. After we checked in at home, Bart set Mika and me up with beds in separate guest rooms. I was practically asleep before my head hit the pillow.

The three of us convened in the lab an hour early and set up chairs by the water cut. We didn't want to take the chance that our estimate of the time for the meeting was inaccurate and find that Leo's mother had been waiting on us. That turned out to be a smart decision because exactly seven minutes after we sat down, Leo and another dolphin quietly surfaced in front of us. We quickly knelt close to the edge of the cut while Mika and Leo made the introductions by means of sign language and dolphin squeaks and clicks.

When Mika introduced Augie to Leo's mom, Augie very formally placed his hands together in the prayer attitude and bowed low. That seemed to delight Leo's mom, who clicked rapidly to her son then bowed – sort of – in return. Augie donned a second brain coupler, which was coded differently from the one Mika wore. This let Augie communicate with Mom, while Mika conversed with Leo. I was content to watch, totally fascinated by the whole thing. Can you imagine speaking with a couple of dolphins as casually as you might sit around a table and chat with your friends? Blows the mind, right?

It was still a bit laborious, like talking with someone from Germany who spoke only a little English, while you only understood a little German. In the end though, Leo's mother gave her consent to the procedure. After another consultation of the tide and current table, we set this evening at quarter after seven as the time for Leo's operation.

Leo and his mom swam away, and the three of us trooped to Augie's kitchen for some of Bart's blueberry pancakes before school. I called Dr. Tim before the first class and asked if he could be back at the lab by seven o'clock.

"Try and keep me away," he said.

## Chapter Twenty-nine

**Augie was dressed** in a white operating gown, complete with surgical mask and clear face shield. He looked like a stand-in for Doogie Howser on the old sit-com, but I didn't bother pointing that out. Dr. Tim was next to him, dressed similarly. Augie maintained that it was actually a simple procedure, to be completed under local anesthetic only, but I was glad my fourth father was there to help.

Mika was also assisting Augie. She was responsible for keeping Leo cool and wet. Just being out of the water was difficult for him. Augie's custom-made cradle provided a lot of support, but it wasn't the same as being supported entirely by the pressure of the ocean around your body. And if he overheated while he was out of the water, Leo could be in serious trouble.

Earlier, Bart and I had rigged up the gurney that Leo was going to be resting on in the waterway that cut into the lab. Another Augie on-the-spot invention, it resembled a miniature boat lift. Two hydraulic arms lowered the special cradle into the water. Leo simply swam into the lift and rested on the padded cradle. Augie used a remote to wirelessly raise the cradle and tilt the whole works over to the side, where it then sat on a special rack that held everything – Leo and the cradle – steady. The whole "operating room" had been surrounded by curtains and was brightly illuminated by overhead lights that Augie had installed earlier.

Augie and Dr. Tim both wore brain couplers so that they could receive thoughts from Leo. And of course, Augie could communicate directly with Leo by sign language. Bart and I sat in chairs on the other side of the glass wall. Mika and I were near the door, in case our help was needed. I could see Leo's mother stick her head up in the water cut now and then. She'd watch for a bit, swim off, then return. Nervous, I thought.

Augie signed to Leo that he was ready. Apparently, Leo gave him permission to begin because Augie picked up a syringe with a long needle and poked it gently into Leo's smooth grey hide. I checked the time and settled in my chair to watch.

Three hours later, Augie was finished. Leo had been given a mild sedative and was drifting into sleep as Mika lowered his cradle into the water. Augie signaled her to stop the cradle when Leo's blow hole was above the surface so that he could relax and breathe. Leo's mother swam in and inspected the arrangement. She squeaked once briefly, and I think Leo woke up long enough to tell her he was fine. He went back to sleep and his mom slipped out the channel.

Dr. Tim stripped off his surgical garb and dumped it in the basket Augie had ready. He gave me a hug and another for Mika. Then he shook Augie's hand in a very formal way.

"Thank you, sir," he said to Augie, "for allowing me the privilege of assisting in the operation. I've been a veterinarian for eighteen years and I believe this will always be the highlight of my career." He let go of Augie's hand and smiled as he shook his head. "Conversing mentally with a dolphin and implanting an artificial larynx so that you can actually talk to him. If I hadn't seen it myself, I would never believe it. I wish I could stick around to hear him talk, but I have a full schedule of operations that I can't miss."

I'm sure that must have been the first time a qualified veterinarian called Augie *sir*, but he accepted it with aplomb. He picked up the brain coupler that Dr. Tim had been wearing during the operation and held it out to him.

"Please accept this as a gift, Dr. Raymond," he said. "We could not have done this without you. Plus, I'm sure that you will put it to good use in your practice."

From the look on his face, Dr. Tim couldn't be happier if the brain coupler had been solid gold. He took it reverently, then placed it back on his head. He shook Augie's hand once more, waved goodbye to the rest of us and walked out of the lab looking like an angel with an electronic halo.

# Chapter Thirty

MIKA AND AUGIE had worked out a schedule so that they could split the time overseeing Leo's recovery, with Mika taking the first shift. I offered to take an equal shift, but Augie argued that I needed to rest since I was the one and only dolphin suit driver. Mika backed him up, but I figured both of them suspected I might have certain shortcomings in the nursing department. They would probably be right. In any event, the entire night passed before Augie was satisfied that Leo was ready to try out his new voice box.

When we were finally ready for the test early Tuesday morning, the weather had turned nasty again. A weather front was driving in from the Pacific Ocean, and the gusting wind was kicking Fidalgo Bay into milky rows of white-capped waves. The tide in the cut was at maximum height, nearly up to the floor of the lab, so whenever a large wave slapped at the entrance to the cut, frothy sea water slopped over the edge and swirled around the floor. Augie, Mika and I were ignoring the occasional overflow, sitting on the floor close to the cut. Leo was floating in the cut, his head out of the water so that he could see us. Augie had the lights turned down very low, in deference to the sensitive eyes of our bottlenose buddy. As I mentioned before, the room in the lab, where the cut was located, was sealed off from the rest of the lab by floor-to-ceiling glass to keep the salt-laden air away from the sensitive equipment. As a result, the air in here was very warm, damp and salty. All three of us humans wore bathing suits, partly because of the warmth, partly because we might have to jump into the cut in case something went wrong and Leo needed assistance. In addition to his bathing suit, Augie was wearing his Akubra hat with the brain coupler. The only way he could have looked sillier was if he added cowboy boots to the outfit.

Augie had apparently given a fair amount of thought as to how Leo should attempt to use his artificial larynx to speak. Mika and I sat quietly while he used sign language to give Leo advice on how to squeeze the larynx with the muscles surrounding his blowhole while simultaneously pushing the correct amount of air through it with his diaphragm. In the end I thought Leo would intuitively have a better feel for how to speak than Augie could ever tell him.

Augie finally finished his primer and signed to Leo that he should give it a try.

Leo just held himself steady for a few moments, then we heard him take in an extra-large lungful of air. He blinked a couple of times, then with a high-pitched, amazingly clear voice he sang, "Well hello, I am Leo."

Yes, he sang! The first words ever spoken by a bottlenose dolphin were a perfect little rhyming ditty, sung in the key of *C*.

Our jaws dropped and then we exploded with laughter. All three of us jumped into the water – OMG was it cold – and we hugged Leo. I'm sure he would have hugged us back if he had the required arms and hands, but he showed his delight with squeals and back flips.

The cold drove us from the water pretty quickly, plus the plight of the next families in the hands of the smugglers was always on our minds. After we had dried off and put on regular clothes, we pulled chairs close to the water and Augie gave Leo his assignment.

"Leo, we need to find out where the submarine comes from and where it goes," Augie said in sign language. "In fact, we need to know all about it. What route does it follow? Is it the same every time? When does it leave and when does it arrive? How deep does it go?"

There was a pause while Leo hyperventilated a little bit. He'd already discovered that he could talk more clearly when he had a big lungful of air to push past the larynx.

"Is . . . that . . . all?" he asked.

Mika and I glanced at each other in surprise. Was this sarcasm? From a dolphin who just learned how to talk? If it was, it flew right over Augie's head.

"Yes," he said. "And can you get all your friends to tell you when they see it?"

Before Leo answered, Mika stepped into his line of sight. She signed something to him, speaking it out loud for my benefit.

"Leo . . . my friend . . ." she signed, "children are in danger. We need to know about this submarine quickly."

Leo took a deep breath. It was probably my imagination, but I thought Leo's dolphin smile had gone away. When Leo let the air out of his lungs, he used it to push one word through his artificial larynx three times: "Quick . . . quick . . . quick!"

Then he flipped over and disappeared through the cut.

# Chapter Thirty-one

LEO WAS AS good as his word. Well, his three words, but they were all the same: *quick*. Our yellow-tailed bottlenose friend was back in the cut early Wednesday morning. Augie, having checked the tides, met him there. Leo told him everything he and his cetacean compadres had discovered about where and when the submarine had been sighted.

The good news was that Leo had collected a lot of good information. It seemed that almost everyone in the dolphin world had seen the sub at one time or another. Augie thought we could pinpoint the sub's location without too much difficulty on its next trip.

The bad news was that Leo and his friends were almost certain that the sub was going to be launched again in less than three hours. That gave us almost no time to prepare. According to Leo, the sub would put to sea somewhere along the Canadian coast near Sidney, British Columbia. Where exactly was unknown, but Leo was certain that the sub would travel down Haro Strait close to Stuart Island, then stay in the deep water north of Spieden Island. If it stayed with the route it had navigated every trip before this one, Leo and his friends thought the sub would cruise down San Juan Channel, turn left through Upright Channel and go around the north end of Lopez Island. It would skirt Leo Reef where we first tested the dolphin suit, then slip out Thatcher Pass and over to the mainland somewhere near Anacortes. That *somewhere near* part of the route was a big problem. There were lots of covered boat yards and commercial docks where they could bring the sub to the surface undetected. We needed to intercept it somewhere between Sidney and Anacortes.

Leo understood the need for speed. He said he would take short cuts through places too shallow for the *Golly Gee* and he'd be waiting for us near Stuart Island. Before he swam off, Leo gave us one more bit of bad news: a large orca with an extremely bad disposition always accompanied the submarine for the entire trip.

I called my dad, who said he had just met with the Coast Guard in Bellingham to ask if one or two of their vessels could help us find the sub. He was on his way to meet with the Anacortes Police who had volunteered the use of their high speed launch.

Using the hands free phone connection in his Dodge Charger, he said, "I didn't think we would need all these vessels right away, but the timing is certainly fortuitous. I'll call the Coast Guard back and get them underway. Meantime, I'm going to take the Anacortes Police up on their offer of a fast boat. Kevin is still available to transport you and the dolphin suit?"

"Yep," I said. "We're on the way to Cap Sante now."

"Good," my dad said. "Keep the radio on. Channel 16, right? I'll catch up to you somewhere along the way."

Kevin had told us he would be ready to go at a moment's notice and he was as good as his word. Twenty minutes after I called, Bart was delivering Augie, Mika and me to the marina again, stuffed into the Mercedes with the disassembled dolphin suit. As we wheeled it – under tarps to avoid drawing unnecessary attention – towards Kevin's boat in the marina's courtesy carts, four guys were headed the other way, grumbling with each other about a cancelled fishing trip.

"Sorry about your charter, dad," I said when we made it down to the *Golly Gee*. This was the first time I'd awarded the *Dad* title to Kevin. Even though he and mom wouldn't be married until next month, I thought he'd earned it. Not just today, but through this entire adventure. He'd always given me and my friends his full attention and never blown us off as kids-doing-kid-stuff.

He gave me a big smile from the fly bridge of his boat and said, "No problem." Then he climbed down the ladder and helped me wrestle the suit from the dock to the deck. When we were all aboard, Kevin sat us down at the little dinette table and spread out a chart of the San Juans. Augie and Mika filled him in on what Leo had told them, tracing their fingers over the chart where Leo thought the sub would be.

When Kevin ran out of questions, he looked at each of us in turn. Then he said, "No time to lose, right? Did you call D-1?"

My first thought was . . . when did my father and stepfathers start calling themselves D-1, D-2 and so on? I liked it. Amusing, but useful.

"Yep," I said. "He's going to catch up to us in the Anacortes Police boat. Plus, he's got the Coast Guard sending at least one vessel out of Bellingham. We're supposed to keep the radio on channel sixteen so he can contact us."

We moved the chart to the fly bridge, then Kevin cranked the engines. He and Mika cast off while Augie and I started getting the dolphin suit ready. About forty-five minutes later, as Augie and I finished preparing the suit, I looked up to see Friday Harbor sliding by on the left side of the boat. We had made excellent time.

Mika suddenly called down from the flybridge to get our attention, then she pointed astern. Turning that way, I saw a boat coming up fast, riding a big white bow wave. It was the Anacortes Police boat, a fiberglass thirty-footer with a center console and a pair of huge outboard engines. A blue light winked steadily from atop the center console as it pulled alongside the *Golly Gee* and the operator throttled back to match our speed.

We were passing through an area that Kevin said the locals called the *Washing Machine*, because underwater currents flowed in from three different directions outside of Friday Harbor and collided to form this patch of nearly continuous lumpy seas. The choppy, confused waves made it tough for my dad, who was braced against the police boat's gunnel and hanging on to the railing on the center console just to stay upright. In his free hand, my dad held the microphone for the police boat's loudhailer.

Kevin eased the *Golly Gee's* throttles back, but my dad's metallic voice said, "Keep going! Keep going! We don't have a minute to lose."

When Kevin was back to cruise speed, the police boat matched it again. My dad tapped the operator on the shoulder, then pointed toward our boat. The police boat slid closer, until we could practically reach across and touch hands. With a larger, heavier hull, the *Golly Gee* was handling the waves better than the police boat.

The loudhailer wasn't needed anymore up this close. We didn't have to shout exactly, just speak loudly. My dad started things off.

"I have some information that you need to hear," he said, "but we can't use the radio because wherever that sub is headed, the gang at that end is sure to be listening with a scanner. We don't want them to drop everything and disappear."

"OK dad," I said, "we can hear you. Go ahead."

The police boat lurched suddenly when it hit one of the Washing Machine's weird waves and my dad had to make a frantic grab for the railing with both hands to avoid getting tossed overboard. He managed to hang on, then a took deep breath and nodded.

"The Canadian police came through for us," he said. "They located a shipping container that was listed with the Customs Service as originating in Fiji. But the documents for the container had been forged. It actually came from Hong Kong."

A wave ran down between our boats and was suddenly squeezed up between the hulls, splashing all of us with cold saltwater. We hardly paid any attention, wiping our faces off as my dad continued.

"It was one of the smaller standard shipping containers. Twenty feet long and eight feet wide. It had been crudely converted into living quarters. A composting toilet, plastic water jugs, ventilation holes, foam pads to sleep on.

Nothing remotely fancy. The Canadians say that thirteen people lived inside for five weeks during the voyage across the Pacific."

If you've been anywhere near a seaport, you've seen those containers. They're taken off ships by big cranes and loaded onto trailers, which are then hooked up to trucks and driven off to Nebraska or New Mexico or wherever the goods inside are destined. I tried to picture thirteen people locked inside one of those dark, stifling boxes for five long weeks as the ship rolled and pitched its way across the ocean. I shook my head at the sheer misery it must have been.

"Do you know who they are?" Augie asked.

My dad nodded.

"They all scratched their names on the inside of the container. And yes, one of the names is Shizuko Li."

"So, she's probably on the submarine?" Augie said. He looked intently at my dad as he said that, and I couldn't say if his expression was one of relief or anxiety. If she was on the sub, at least we knew where she was now. On the other hand, everyone on that sub was in danger.

My dad nodded again, his mouth set in a grim line.

"We think all thirteen are on the sub," he said. He paused and motioned to the police boat operator to move a little closer. I think he wanted to make sure all of us on the *Golly Gee* understood what he was going to say next.

"The Canadian police rounded up four gang members in Sidney. None of them is saying a word. We're still searching for the gang at our end. The Anacortes Police have two boats out and the Lummi Indian Police have another three. But the landing point for the sub could be out of sight, in a private boathouse. We're still working on search warrants. But here's the thing: the Canadian police think the gang members are all hoping that we won't catch the submarine, because without the testimony of the passengers who are on that sub right now, they have a good chance of going free."

"Well that . . ." I said.

"Sucks," Mika finished for me.

My dad didn't bother to correct her language.

"Yeah, it sucks all right," he said. "But it gets even worse."

"How could it get worse?" Augie cried.

"The gang in Sidney burned a bunch of stuff that might have incriminated them, but the Canadians managed to save part of a mechanical drawing. They said it shows an escape hatch for the operator of the sub. They think it's possible that the sub operator might try to ditch the sub and escape with scuba gear."

We were stunned to silence as we tried to absorb that terrible news. Finally Mika spoke for all of us.

"But then everyone in the sub would die!" she said.

"Yeah," my father said. "Those poor folks would die, and the crooks would get away." He dropped his head for a moment, then looked up at us. "You've got to find a way to force that sub to the surface," he said. "Fast."

He pulled himself back against the police boat's center console and signaled to the boat's driver to steer away from the *Golly Gee*.

"I'll bring the Coast Guard," my dad shouted as the police boat accelerated ahead. "You get that sub!"

Kevin pushed the Golly Gee's throttles forward and the

boat shuddered as it struggled up to its maximum speed. We watched the police boat as it turned up President Channel and sped northeast along Orcas Island.

Kevin said, "Your dad is going that way to hook up with the Coast Guard from Bellingham. It'll be at least an hour before they get back. Probably more." He looked us over, his face the same grim mask my father's had been. "We're on our own until then."

I think he saw a crew of kids determined not to fail, because he nodded quickly and said, "I'll run up the north side of Spieden Island as fast as the *Golly Gee* can go. You three make sure the dolphin suit is ready to go. I'll stop as soon as we get to Stuart Island. You said Leo would meet us there. I hope he's on time."

He held up a fist and we each bumped it before climbing down the flybridge ladder. Fifteen minutes later, we cleared Spieden Island and saw Stuart Island directly in front of the *Golly Gee*. Kevin pulled the throttles back and let the boat drift to a stop. Leo appeared at the stern almost immediately. Kevin cut the engines so that we could all hear what Leo had to say.

Leo blew a lungful of air out of his larynx to clear it of any water. Then he took another deep breath and said, "Sub . . . here . . . quick."

Augie reached up and put a hand on my shoulder.

"Time to suit up, Coop."

# Chapter Thirty-two

IN AUGIE'S DOLPHIN suit, I followed Leo into the cold depths, grateful for the bright yellow color of the appendage that Augie had given him. Leo looked back – dolphins are surprisingly flexible in the neck area – and gave an emphatic click that I could actually hear underwater as it pinged off my helmet. Then he nosed over and headed down. I had heard the click, but of course I couldn't understand Leo's language of clicks and squeals. I assumed he said something like "Follow me!" so I pushed my own nose over and hit the throttle.

The southwest side of Stuart Island is a steep rockface, especially at the northern end of the island where the Turn Point lighthouse is located. Underwater, the slope is basically a continuation of what you see on the land. You could practically jump from the shore into a hundred and fifty fathoms of water. For the landlubbers, that's nine hundred feet. The deep end of the pool, for sure.

Leo swam straight down. I stayed right on his tail, with one eye on the depth readout. Thirty feet. Fifty. Eighty. One ten. One fifty. One eighty. Two ten. Right about there

I could almost hear Kevin whisper in my ear, "Beyond two hundred feet, I can't rescue you with scuba gear." Two fifty. Two ninety. I was starting to wish I had a leash on Leo when he abruptly leveled out. My heads up display read exactly three hundred feet.

It was dark down here.

Leo stopped in front of me, close enough for the brain coupler to work. I pulled the trigger to activate it and felt that now familiar tug inside my head that meant Leo was with me.

"Sub," was the only thing on his mind. He did a quick flip and came to a stop with his nose facing slightly ahead and down. I looked in the direction he indicated.

Nothing.

No, wait. A shadow. My eyes were adapting to the low light now. I was definitely seeing something moving.

It had to be the sub. Man, it was big. The thing came closer, still hidden in the gloom but now I could make out the general shape of it.

Suddenly Leo started squealing and clicking like crazy. He just had time to mentally shout, "Look out!" when something huge blew past me at ninety miles an hour and sent me tumbling. It didn't actually hit me, but then it didn't need to. Something that big, moving that fast, that close . . . well, all I can say is this thing pushed a wall of water the way a hurricane pushed a wall of air.

The orca had arrived. Not actually at ninety miles an hour of course, but fast. OMG, so fast. I was a hundred feet away and thirty feet deeper before I could get the dolphin suit under control.

I looked around wildly, trying to orient myself. The

sub was out of sight and the water around me appeared uniformly dark. As I turned my head, I felt the leather thong holding the vegvisir around my neck. Hoping the Vikings had been right about that thing pointing the way. I turned west. The sub appeared out of the gloom. I smiled, then wondered about the next step. If the vegvisir will help you get where you gotta go, will it help you figure out what to do when you get there?

I hit the throttle and made straight for the sub. Before I reached it, the orca cruised up alongside me with no apparent effort, like we were enjoying a friendly stroll in the park. It looked me over with a big black eye. I wondered if it was admiring Augie's dolphin suit or analyzing it for weak points. The answer came when the orca casually rolled over and rammed into me.

Want an idea how it feels to be body slammed by an adult orca? Walk out to the freeway and throw yourself against the side of the first fully loaded dump truck that roars by. Without the protection of Augie's dolphin suit, that killer whale would have killed me.

I checked myself over mentally and didn't feel anything that was broken. Hurting, yes; but thankfully not broken. The suit withstood the orca's attack even better than I had. Everything was functioning normally. I hightailed it back toward the sub. As I reached it, the orca reached me.

This guy – I could tell it was a guy orca by the very tall dorsal fin – was a smart guy. One attempt to put me out of commission by ramming was all it took for him to decide that technique wasn't going to work. This time he swooped at me just as fast, but at the last second he dove under me.

That tall dorsal fin I'd been admiring nearly chopped me in two.

Fortunately, I remembered what Mika had said about the orca harassing the Lummi Canoe Festival: *it was almost like he used his dorsal fin as a weapon.* This had to be the same animal, right? I mean what were the chances of two killer whales going rogue at the same time?

The instant before the orca dove under me, I arched my back as hard as I could, kicked my feet elevators up and did the world's first underwater backflip in a dolphin suit. Still, the orca was so fast that the tip of his dorsal fin caught my shoulder and sent me spinning as well as flipping. Before I could get myself stopped and reoriented, he was on me again.

This time he opened his mouth and latched on to the left leg of my suit. I didn't dare kick out because I was afraid all those sharp teeth in the orca's powerful jaw would chew right through the suit. I was lifted like a rag doll by the orca, who dragged me toward the surface.

Leo zoomed up, sprinting to stay close. I keyed the coupler. Leo's brain shot one crystal clear thought into mine: "We coming!"

If dolphins could ride horses, they would have been the cavalry. Bunches of them charged in from every direction, ramming and biting at the orca. Not just Leo's bottlenose dolphin family either. A pod of harbor porpoises zipped into the fight. They concentrated their efforts on the orca's fins, biting and pulling in concert like they had rehearsed this kind of thing before.

The orca tossed me aside and turned to deal with the dolphins. When I say *turned*, I mean *spun*. It was like seeing a Greyhound bus tuck itself into a tight ball, whip around and straighten out. The orca charged after the retreating pod of dolphins and with three quick flicks of its powerful tailfin caught the straggler of the bunch. The poor dolphin squealed and clicked in heartrending desperation. A dark cloud spread around the orca's jaws where it gripped the dolphin by one of its pectoral fins. It looked black at this depth, but I knew it was red.

Leo streaked past my head. Like last time he managed only to transmit one urgent thought to me: "Mom!"

# Chapter Thirty-three

**WITHOUT ANY CONSCIOUS** thought, I yanked the throttle full on. I lowered my arms and straightened my legs to get as streamlined as possible. There was an agonizing pause while Augie's incredible drive system ramped up to full power, then I shot towards the orca like a Polaris missile.

The orca was swimming slowly now. It had Leo's mother in its jaws and was broadside to me, intent on luring us away from the sub. The orca's huge black body blended with the dark background, but its white chin and the white stripe over its eye glowed brightly, giving me a good target. From this distance the orca seemed to be grinning, but I could swear that the one eye that was pointed toward me grew big and round in alarm when it saw how fast I was coming.

Fifty feet . . . forty . . . twenty. I stayed on the throttle. My heads up display read thirty knots. This was going to be a colossal collision. I hoped that Augie had built the same extraordinary strength into the helmet of this suit that he had put in all of his other inventions. I aimed just behind the orca's eye, which now looked the size of a dinner plate.

Wham!

It was like a train wreck underwater. The impact shoved me forward in the suit, slamming my shoulders against the frame. The top of my head hit the inside of the helmet, nearly knocking me out. My vision went fuzzy, with shooting stars around the edges. I shook my head to clear it, just in time to see the orca open its mouth and Leo's mom dart away.

My finger was still on the throttle, holding me against the orca. The ends of the dolphin suit's arms were fitted with fins, not hands, so I couldn't grab hold of the orca. But I could bend my arms and legs, so I did the next best thing. I cut the throttle and quickly rolled on top of the orca, stuffing one arm in each side of its open mouth and wrapping my legs around its body. I levered my arms tightly inside its jaw, behind the rows of teeth.

The orca stayed absolutely motionless for one stunned instant, then it went berserk.

I pulled myself even tighter onto its back, like a cowboy coming out of the chute on the world's meanest bucking bronco. The killer whale jinked left then right, rolled dizzyingly through four or five complete revolutions. That didn't dislodge me, so it somersaulted through a couple of vicious outside loops. I hung on, wishing for spurs and a saddle. The orca rolled onto its back and shook its head. It shook so hard a shudder like an earthquake trembled through its entire body. When the quake stopped, I was still there.

With a couple of powerful flicks of its tail, the orca pointed itself straight up toward the surface. For an instant we hung motionless in the sea. An image popped unbidden into my head and I'm sure it didn't come from Leo: Cape

Kennedy, with the space shuttle and its solid rocket boosters lifting off on a huge ball of flame.

The orca paused for a second, maybe to gather its strength, then streaked straight for the sun. My stomach was left far behind as I hung on desperately. For the second time in my short life I erupted out of the ocean in Augie's dolphin suit.

The orca's aerial maneuver worked perfectly, at least from the orca's point of view. We sailed out of the water, arced over gracefully and re-entered with a tremendous splash. Unfortunately, the object that generated most of the splash was me. To say I was separated from the orca would be a gross understatement. I was forcefully blown off. My head slammed so hard against the inside of the helmet I was knocked out.

I regained consciousness a short time later – it couldn't have been more than a minute – surrounded by soft green light filtered by the sea. Leo and his twin were staring at me. If they got any closer, they'd have to come inside the suit. I shook my head again, a mistake in terms of pain, but it cleared my double vision. Leo was just one dolphin again.

The HUD was still functioning properly, and I saw that I was drifting only a few feet below the surface.

Leo beamed "OK?" into my head.

When I nodded – carefully this time – he beamed "Whale gone!"

I beamed back "Where's the sub?"

Leo flipped over without hesitation and darted downward. I pushed my pain aside, shot to the surface for a quick breath of fresh air and dove after his bright yellow tail.

# Chapter Thirty-four

THE SUB WAS still running at three hundred feet, making good time toward its destination near Anacortes. Now that I could take a good look at it, one thing was immediately certain: Leo wasn't far off when he described the sub as the biggest, meanest fish in the ocean.

You've gotta remember that objects look almost one third bigger underwater than they really are. This is because light gets bent slightly – refracted is Augie's more preferred scientific term – as it passes from the water in the ocean to the air in your mask. Or in my helmet in this case. So I gotta tell you, that refracted sub looked humongous. It was probably only fifty feet long, not too much bigger than the *Golly Gee*, but how many fifty-foot critters do you ever see underwater?

I say critter because as I got closer, I could see that it had huge round eyes, dark circles about two feet in diameter that stared at you with the merciless concentration of a hungry tiger shark. I moved up parallel with the beast and when I was within thirty feet of its head, I realized that the circles weren't eyes after all. Yeah, I'll admit it, my imagination does tend to charge off on its own now and then. The circles turned out to be viewing ports, one on each side of the sub, way up toward the bow. I knew they were viewing ports because from this close I could see the sub's operator behind the glass.

His face was illuminated by the lights from an instrument panel of some kind in front of him. He had a long pointy nose, short reddish hair and a pointy goatee. He was wearing gold framed glasses and when he saw me zooming along just outside, his eyes suddenly got as big as the viewing ports. His hands were on a steering yoke, similar to the type you might find in a small plane. After he'd collected his wits, he twisted the yoke violently to the right.

The sub heeled over with impressive speed, far more maneuverable than I would have guessed for such a large vessel. When the operator yanked on the wheel, I could see an array of winglets just behind the viewing ports, rotate upward in unison. There were three of them, stacked one over the other, and they seemed to work like ailerons on an airplane, causing the sub to roll quickly and change direction. As I dodged away from the sub, I thought the thing really did look like a huge fish, with viewing ports that suggested eyes and winglets that resembled gills.

The operator was going wild, trying to smash the sub into me. For a few minutes we rolled and dived and climbed like a couple of biplanes in a dogfight. I think he finally realized that my dolphin suit was far more maneuverable than his sub. He leveled out at one hundred and thirty feet and turned back on his original course, so I risked coming alongside again to examine the rest of the sub. The bottom wasn't flat, but it wasn't exactly round either. Sort of like a big pipe that had been flattened into an elliptical shape. The sub was so narrow at the bow that there was just enough room for the operator. Then it widened out for the main body, which looked about six feet wide and maybe five feet high. There were no viewing ports on the main body, but I figured that everyone must be sitting inside that part of the sub.

I slowed a bit, so that I could slip back toward the stern of the craft. About twenty feet back from the bow, the body of the sub gradually flattened even more, until near the stern it resembled a squat wing.

With Leo and another fifteen or twenty of his compadres in tow, I carefully inspected the entire exterior of the sub. It took me about twenty minutes, in part because I had to break off three times and surface to suck some fresh air into the suit. Every time I came close to the viewing ports, I checked to be sure the operator was still at the controls of the sub. I was deathly afraid that he might decide to use the escape hatch the Canadian police had told my dad about. If he grabbed his scuba gear and ejected himself somehow, the sub would flood and head straight for the bottom. I'd never be able to save the people inside.

But I figured he must not know that his Canadian friends had been captured because each time I came around he was still at the controls. He shouted at me, not that I could hear him. But I'm pretty sure he was shouting at me since I could see him open his mouth wide and shake his fist. I *am* sure he kept swerving to try and ram me at every opportunity. I was getting pretty nimble with the dolphin suit by now though and he never came close.

What I was looking for was a handle. Not an actual

handle, of course, but some way that I could grab the sub and force it up. I spent a long time looking at the propeller and rudder at the stern. The problem was that the propeller was recessed into a shroud that also supported the rudder. Augie would probably have pointed out the ways that this arrangement made the sub both quiet and quick, but all I knew was that I couldn't get a grip on the sub's rear end. If I stuck my arm into that whirling prop, I was certain it would cut my arm off, dolphin suit or no dolphin suit.

Finally, I remembered something my dad had written in his notes while he was using Augie's brain coupler with the kid in the coma. The kid had been thinking about being swallowed by a whale. I realized that crew members entered a regular submarine through the conning tower, but this sub didn't have one. Maybe the whole bow was hinged to swing down while it was out of the water so that people could enter. If that was the case, there might be some part of the hinge mechanism that I could use.

I surfaced for one more quick exchange of air in the suit so that I'd have as much oxygen available as possible, then I angled straight back down to the sub. I matched the sub's speed when I approached the bow, then slipped underneath.

Sure enough, up near the bow on the underside of the sub there was a slot about a foot long and maybe two inches wide. The arm that supported the bow must move into that slot when the bow is lowered, but I had another use for it. I was going to jam the dolphin suit's dorsal fin into the slot and attach myself to the sub like a remora. I had to smile when I remembered that Augie had etched a vegvisir onto the dorsal fin. Maybe the vegvisir actually *could* help you figure out what to do when you arrived at your destination. Then again, maybe I was finally thinking on my feet like my dad said. Or on my fins.

I eased under the sub and raised myself up slowly. I couldn't see the slot, but Leo immediately caught on to my plan.

He beamed "Back up." into my head.

I adjusted with the throttle and let myself slide back in relation to the sub.

"Back more."

I eased back a fraction more.

"You're good to go."

Well, I don't suppose Leo actually used the phrase "You're good to go," but something like that zipped into my brain.

I used my legs and hand fins to raise myself up while keeping level. There was a *click* when the tip of my dorsal fin touched the sub.

Leo beamed "Wait," then a second later, "OK."

He must have guided my fin into the slot with his nose because when I raised myself up again, I felt the fin wedge itself into the slot.

"Hah!" I said to myself. "Take that, you mad killer whale. I'm stealing your trick and using my dorsal fin for something it was never designed to do."

I was part of the sub now, for better or worse. The *better* part would be if I had enough power in this suit to force the sub to the surface. The *worse* part was that I would get no more fresh air until someone got me out of this suit. Even when the sub was at the surface, I would be underwater. In just a few minutes I was going to use up all the oxygen in the suit if I couldn't get to the surface.

I took a deep breath of my precious air to clear my head, then I pulled the throttle on. My legs flopped out to the sides as the thrust built. I cut the power and thought it through. If I could have slapped my forehead and said *doh!* in Homer Simpson's voice, I would have. I was anchored to an object the size of a bus and I was trying to change its direction. My legs were like my steering wheel; I'd have to keep them pointed where I wanted the sub to go. I pressed my knees together, wished I'd done more sit-ups like I'd promised myself last New Year's Eve and clenched my stomach muscles. I eased the power steadily on. My legs jumped and twisted at first, but I kept them under control. I pointed my feet down, trying to push the nose of the sub up.

The HUD read one hundred twenty feet. We were ascending! I squeezed the throttle on a fraction more. I pushed down for all I was worth, but the slipstream of water slapped my heels against the hull. I extended my arms to get as much help as possible from the hand fins and kicked down with my legs. I contracted every muscle I had to keep them down. I curled my finger until the throttle maxed out. After thirty seconds I was drenched in sweat. It poured out of me like I was a sponge in some giant's hand. After a minute my abs were screaming and my thighs ached. The HUD said one hundred and ten.

Too deep. Too slow. I wasn't going to make it.

I felt a bump against my chest, then a vibration.

Like a hard flutter.

Then another bump.

More fluttering.

Then Leo appeared in front of my face. Can dolphins wink? I'd swear he winked just before he twirled around with the incredible underwater grace of his species and pressed his belly against my helmet. I looked down and could see Leo's powerful prosthetic tail hammering through the water. The bumps I felt must have been his friends doing the same all around me.

A wave of exhilaration passed through me. My fatigue vanished. I did the mother of all stomach crunches and ratcheted my legs another couple of degrees lower. The power unit in Augie's suit started howling. Red warning bars flashed on both sides of the HUD. It read ninety feet now and the climb rate was increasing.

Eighty-eight. Eighty-five.

The red bars were replaced with one large yellow word: OVERHEAT. Seventy-two feet. Sixty- six. The OVER-HEAT warning changed color from yellow to red. Then it began pulsing on and off. It felt like Augie was down here yelling at me in person.

Fifty feet.

I kept my finger locked on the throttle lever. The howl of the suit's propulsion unit turned to a metallic screech. More bumps rocked me. I hoped it was more of Leo's friends adding their muscle to the effort and not pieces flying off the dolphin suit.

Thirty-five feet.

We were climbing more rapidly toward the surface now.

Twenty-five.

If Augie's suit held together, I'd have the sub at the

surface in less than a minute. The watery world around me was getting brighter. There was no chance we'd breach in a spectacular fashion like I'd done with the orca and the run-away suit, but still . . . that sub weighed many tons and it was going to suddenly surface. If something that big – running at somewhere between ten and fifteen miles an hour – hits a boat, the result could only be disaster. I hoped Augie, Mika and Kevin had managed to clear the way.

The red OVERHEAT display started flashing faster and the howling inside the suit faded into an even more ominous grinding noise. The dolphin suit was seconds away from complete failure.

## Chapter Thirty-five

**SUNLIGHT AT LAST!** I could feel the sub break the surface because it suddenly began tossing slightly in the waves. I released the throttle and the red warning lights blinked off. I was still trapped beneath the bow, the dorsal fin of my suit wedged into the docking slot. I shoved up and down with my arms and legs, trying to work myself free. No go.

Oxygen was in short supply in the suit. I'd used up most of it working so hard to get the sub to the surface and now the air I was sucking in and out of my lungs had too little of the precious stuff left. I was wheezing like a black-smith's worn out bellows, straining for every life-giving molecule. Five feet above me there was an endless supply of nice fresh air, richly laden with nearly 21% oxygen. Five feet. It might as well have been five miles.

The sub was still driving itself along at full speed. About ten or twelve miles an hour I thought. Not that fast as far as boats in general go, but downright speedy for a homemade submarine. I couldn't see him from my position locked under the bow of the sub, but I imagined that the operator was cursing up a storm. I could feel him zigzagging back and forth, trying his best to dislodge me.

I could also feel the vibration of the sub's electric motor and hear its high-pitched whining. I knew I was stuck down here until they got the thing stopped somehow. I tried to ration myself with shallow breaths, but the air rasped down my throat with each rise and fall of my chest.

My vision started closing in around the edges.

The sub's motor screeched and howled, then suddenly died.

The whole world jerked to a stop.

I passed out.

# Chapter Thirty-six

**NEXT THING I** knew I was on my back in the cockpit of the *Golly Gee*, wearing an oxygen mask. Two strangers wearing paramedic uniforms were leaning over me. Mika elbowed them aside, her worried eyes glistening. My mom and all my fathers had told me something at various times over the last three years. They had all used slightly different words, but their message was the same: *your first love never lasts.* If Hallmark made that into a birthday card for teenagers, I would have gotten a slew of them. But when I saw Mika just now, every fiber in my being hoped that was not true.

She smiled, a perfect angel's smile, and said, "I hope you're not brain damaged, cause you can't afford it." Then she raised her head, stuck her fingers in her mouth and let loose a piercing whistle that felt like it drilled a hole in my otherwise undamaged brain. "He's back," she yelled to the world, "Most of him anyway."

I spent the next ten minutes being measured, probed and examined from one end to the other by the paramedics until they were satisfied. After warning me to take it easy for the next few days, they re-boarded their own boat, a big steel Coast Guard cutter that was tied up on *Golly Gee's* port side.

People crowded around me now, and hands helped me sit up.

I found Mika's face again and asked, "How did I get up here?"

"Kevin came up with the plan to stop the sub as soon as you got it to the surface," she said. "He ran to the bow of *Golly Gee* and had me maneuver right up to the stern of the sub. While I held the boat close to the sub, Kevin swung his anchor right into the sub's propeller blades. Chain and all. The sub's motor tried to wind up a hundred fifty feet of heavy chain with a big steel anchor attached to the end. The result was pretty much an instant stop."

I searched for Kevin's face and finally found him looking over Augie's shoulder. He pushed through the crowd and hugged me tightly.

"Great job, Coop, just great," he said.

I hugged him back and said, "You too, Kevin. Uh, dad."

My detective dad climbed over to our boat from the police boat that was tied up on the starboard side. He gave me another big hug.

He said, "They're all safe, Coop. Five families were crammed in that little sub, five moms and eight kids. They're all safe, thanks to you and your friends."

He moved out of the way and I saw them; all standing at the rail of the Coast Guard cutter wrapped in those silver Mylar rescue blankets. Augie was reaching over the flybridge railing to hold hands with one of them: a slender young girl that I thought was probably Shizuko, Augie's online chess partner. Both of them were nodding their heads, smiling and crying all at the same time, which I figured was a reaction to the stress they'd been under and to finding each other safe.

Another of the kids saw me and let out a shout. They all waved like crazy, then they stopped and bowed together. I bowed back as best I could from the stretcher. They waved again, smiling and laughing now as they were herded inside the cutter by a Coast Guard officer.

"They wouldn't budge until they knew that you were all right," my dad said. Then he punched me lightly on the shoulder. "I'm proud of you," he said.

He stepped back and hugged Mika and Augie. Kevin missed out on the hug but got a dad-to-dad handshake. Or maybe it was a detective-to-captain handshake.

"Thanks to all of you," he said, "the Canadian police have arrested four members of the gang in British Columbia and we've rounded up three other members of the gang in Anacortes." He nodded toward the Coast Guard cutter and added, "Plus the driver of the sub, of course." We all looked in that direction in time to see a couple of blue-uniformed Coast Guardsmen slapping handcuffs on the pointy-nosed, goatee-faced sub operator. I noticed he wasn't doing any yelling or cursing now.

My dad smiled as they marched the operator through an open door on the main deck. Then he turned his attention back to us and said, "One last thing. The boy in the coma? I showed his photo to the group from the sub. One of the mothers recognized him right away. His name's Huan Kho. One of the gang members from Canada is cooperating and gave up the location where Huan's parents and the rest of the fathers are being held. The FBI has finally pitched in and they already have a couple of teams headed that way. We'll get these families back together as soon as we possibly can. Incidentally, I was told a few hours ago that Huan was showing signs of coming out of the coma."

My dad gave us all a quick thumbs up, then climbed into the police boat. The blue light on the roof flashed, its twin outboards came to life and the boat took off like any police vehicle – fast.

A commercial towboat had been called to tow the sub and they'd just finished hooking up. As they got underway, the Coast Guard cutter released their lines from our boat and followed the towboat. In the silence that followed, Augie climbed down from the flybridge where he'd been talking with Kevin and Mika.

I stood up as he approached. We both smiled and simultaneously reached out for a quick hug.

"Sorry about the suit," I said.

We walked over to where it had been irreverently propped against the transom. It turned out that Kevin had jumped in the water when they got the sub stopped. He'd wedged himself between the sub and the dolphin suit and used the power in his leg muscles to unjam the dorsal fin. Man, did I owe him for that. The dorsal fin was bent, both arms of the suit had been mangled by the orca's jaws and the ends of the legs looked like they'd been scorched in a hot fire. Before, the suit had always looked alive, shimmering with energy. Now . . . well, now it looked dead.

When I said so, Augie waved that thought away.

"I'll make another," he said. "A better one. But listen Coop, there is someone else who wants to know you're OK." He motioned for Mika to join us, then arranged the three of us at the stern, standing on the dive platform. Augie crouched cautiously, then splashed his hand about in the water. After a few seconds he stood, drying his hand on his pant leg.

Leo's head popped up just behind the boat. Maybe it was just the joyous squeals and clicks that he was making, but his dolphin smile seemed even larger than usual. Another dolphin surfaced next to him, moving much more slowly, but gamely smiling too. Leo's mother, I was certain.

"She's going to swim into the lab on her own this evening," Augie said. "I'll give her a new pectoral fin to replace the one damaged by the orca."

I put my hands together and bowed to her, which brought a low squeal and a melodic whistle in return. I didn't need Augie's brain coupler to know that meant "Thank you."

As she tipped her head in a dolphin bow and slipped away, I was suddenly aware that dozens of sleek cetacean heads were bobbing in the water around the stern of the boat. Most were bottlenose dolphins, but there were several other species as well. It looked like the swimming pool at a birthday party where all the guests got thrown in. Everybody looked happy.

I felt Mika's hand on my shoulder. "Lean close to Leo," she said. "He's got something to tell you."

I looked at her to see what this was all about, but she wouldn't give anything away. I glanced at Augie, who simply smiled and tilted his head toward the water. I knelt on the edge of the dive platform and lowered my head as much as possible. Leo eased over next to me, treading water to keep his head above the surface, although I'm not sure that the clumsy term *treading water* applies to any swimming a dolphin might do.

Using his artificial larynx, Leo said, "My friends . . . and I . . . make you . . . honorary dolphin." He slipped lower into the water and clicked rapidly. Apparently, he was translating what he had just said to me to his friends, because they responded with an enthusiastic clamor of clicks and squeals.

Leo raised himself up again, took another deep breath and continued, "We celebrate . . . you in songs . . . for all time."

I rocked back on my heels in astonishment as the water erupted in the dolphin version of cheers and clapping. Leo flipped over and disappeared, and all of his friends went with him. I knew what was next, so I stood quickly and looked intently down into the water.

"What did he say?" Kevin shouted from the flybridge.

I grinned as I saw Leo and the whole herd charging up from below.

"They made me an honorary dolphin!" I shouted back. "Leo says they'll sing about me forever!"

Leo and the pack burst from the water, the top of their leap even with my head. I reached out with both hands to high five as many fins as I could before I fell laughing into the ocean with my new family.

It's true, you know, the water is so cold up here that your goose bumps have goose bumps.

## Chapter Thirty-seven

SCHOOL THE NEXT morning was interesting to say the least. The story had been all over the news and kids that wouldn't have given Augie a second glance yesterday now vied ferociously for a chance to talk to him or even walk next to him in the hallway. I was happy to see that Augie was being escorted by none other than George Banner, who had flipped from being Augie's personal bully to his personal bodyguard. Just as classes were about to begin Mrs. T called the three of us, Augie, Mika and me, into her office.

Before we sat down, Mika asked, "But Mrs. Treneger, what about chemistry class? I think we're having a surprise quiz on the elements of the Periodic Table."

Mrs. T dismissed Mika's question with a wave of her talons, I mean fingers. Then she invited us to sit. I was a bit stunned to find that the Alcatraz Torture Chairs in front of her desk had been replaced by comfortable-looking wooden chairs with padded seats. As we planted our rear ends down, Mrs. T said, "Now give. Don't leave anything out."

We didn't, but Mika missed the chemistry quiz.

The next day was Saturday, a gorgeous sunny day that makes us Anacortesinians instantly forget about all the drizzly days that came before. D-2 called while mom, Kevin and I were having breakfast on the back porch. I haven't introduced my second dad, have I? His name is Trace Gibson and he lives on the south side of Seattle in a little town called Puyallup. He customizes cars and trucks for a living; usually cool rides like Camaros and Mustangs, but he can also turn a four door Oldsmobile clunker into a high powered work of art. The really neat thing is that instead of replacing the engine with a five hundred horse-power V-8, he ditches the gasoline and installs five hundred electric ponies.

Anyway, apparently Trace had been talking to my detective dad about our recent adventure and he desperately wanted to meet Augie. He was convinced that Augie could help with the battery situation in his electric vehicles, which I'm sure is true. I called Augie who said he's working on another project, but he'd been glad to take a break and meet Trace.

Not being one to waste an opportunity, Trace drove up in his latest project, stopping first at the Seattle police building to pick up D-1. Mika called me in the meantime, and when she heard what was going on, she wanted in. So we looped up to Lummi Island before heading over to Augie's and picked her up. Trace's new project car turned out to be a 2008 Dodge Magnum that he'd picked up at the estate sale after a prominent Seattle art collector passed away. When we got to Mika's, she took one look at Trace's Magnum and said it looked more like a hearse than a car, which got big grins from all of us.

"Give me a couple of months," Trace said graciously, "and I'll show you the first car you want to own when you get a driver's license."

Mika looked doubtful, but she climbed into the back seat with me anyway. We drove straight from Lummi Island to Anacortes and found Augie in the driveway between his house and his lab, setting up some kind of bulky apparatus on a tripod. Bart stood next to him, protecting Augie and his gear from the sun with an oversized umbrella with brightly colored panels that made it look like half of a gigantic beach ball.

When Augie saw us drive up, he motioned for Trace to park in the driveway, with the nose of the car about ten feet away from his tripod. After we got out, I made the introductions all around. We were all so obviously intrigued with Augie's new apparatus that any thought of discussing car batteries was temporarily cast aside.

The thing was perched on a heavy duty tripod and had a Canon lens stuck to the front. I say this with confidence, not because I'm an expert on photographic equipment but because I could see the markings on the lens: *Canon Zoom Lens EF 24-105mm*. As for the rest of the apparatus, I didn't have a clue. I figured it must be a camera since it had that lens, but it didn't look like a camera at all.

For one thing, I'd never seen a camera with a thick power cable. This device had one that ran across the pavement and into Augie's lab. The unit itself was nearly cubical, about two feet on a side. An array of antennas was fastened to each side of the thing, at least I think they were antennas because of their dish-like shape. A large panel full of switches and LED lights had been fastened to the top;

while the entire back was taken up by a large screen. An image of the Dodge Magnum was showing on the screen, confirming my guess that this thing was a camera of some sort. Mika asked the question that all of us had on our lips.

"Is that a camera or what?" she said.

Augie grinned and made a bowing, sweeping gesture like a circus ringmaster introducing the next act.

He said, "I call this my history camera."

"Because it's an antique?" I said, thinking maybe Augie had stuck a new lens on some old, clunky camera body he'd found.

"No Coop, no," Augie said. "I call it my history camera because it can photograph the past."

None of us said a word. I mean, what do you say when you hear something so far out?

Augie just smiled and said, "Allow me to demonstrate."

He stepped back behind the camera and fussed with a few dials. After a minute he asked Mika, Bart and me to set up the scanners that had been stacked on the side of the driveway. They were mounted on tripods like the camera, but much lighter, and each one had an antenna fastened on top. Each of us picked one up and moved it where Augie directed.

"One on each side of the car, please," he said. "And one directly behind." Augie checked his display panel, then handed a tiny scanner on a miniature tripod to Trace and asked him to place it inside the car, on the dashboard.

When everything was set as he wanted, Augie said, "Let me explain how this camera works." He paused and I realized he was mentally translating his explanation into a language we could understand. He gave a little nod after a moment and then said, "As Detective Cooperlick knows, all of us leave a trail of evidence everywhere we go. We leave footprints, tiny fibers from our clothes, and even bits of our DNA. That physical evidence can be collected and analyzed to confirm our presence someplace and even to reconstruct what we did while we were there."

My dad said, "That's right. Everybody leaves evidence behind wherever they go, and if we look hard enough we can find it."

Augie nodded in thanks, then said, "I've discovered that all of us also leave tiny bits of energy everywhere we go, much the same way that we leave physical evidence. And like the physical evidence of our presence, those bits of energy remain long after we are gone. I call it our "energy shadow" because it settles down over time, compressed into a thin, nearly undetectable layer. Wherever we go, we leave an energy shadow; perhaps on the ground or the floor, or even in a car. My scanners detect that energy shadow, amplify it and transmit it to my camera."

"I get that," Mika said, "but say your camera detects the energy shadow where I was standing an hour ago. How can that flat shadow produce a photo of me standing up?"

Augie said, "The computer in my camera un-compresses that shadow. You know those 3D children's books or the 3D greeting cards? The way a scene pops up when you open the pages? Vastly simplified, that's the way my camera works."

"So when you take a photo . . ." Mika said slowly.

Augie nodded quickly and finished for her, "It shows a complete scene from the past."

"How far in the past?" my biodad asked.

Before he answered, Augie showed us the controls on the back of the camera.

"I can put the date I want in here," he said pointing at one of the display panels. "Of course, the further back in time we go, the more faded the image will be."

"See that dent in the hood of the car?" Trace asked. "That happened the day that I bought it, six months ago. Can you set the controls of your history camera back say . . . a year? The dent should be gone in that photo. We could use that as a test."

"Excellent!" Augie said. "Let's do it."

As we watched, he set the controls to today's date, but back one year. Then he pushed the shutter release and took the photo. The image came up slowly on the screen, taking nearly a full minute to come to complete resolution. The dent in the hood was indeed gone, but to our surprise someone was sitting in the driver's seat, looking right at the camera.

"That can't be," my detective dad said.

Augie frowned, then checked the settings on the back of the camera.

"I'm sure we have the date set properly," he said.

"No, it's not your camera," my dad said in his best Detective Cooperlick voice. "It's that man. I recognize him. He was a dangerous felon. In fact, he was on the FBI's ten most wanted list."

"Was?" Augie said.

My dad nodded, his eyes narrowed as he continued to gaze at the image on Augie's camera display. He said, "They reported him dead two years ago."

No one reacted at first. When we realized the meaning

of what my dad just said, we all turned toward him with our mouths hanging open in astonishment.

Except for Augie.

Augie was focused on the photo, one hand at the side of his head as he tapped his temple lightly with one finger. I recognized it as Augie's thinking pose.

Mika had also seen the intensity of Augie's gaze. She looked at me and nodded, a glow of anticipation in her eyes. Both of us knew that Augie was off and running with this new mystery.

"Oh boy," I said, "here we go again."

*Special thanks to Kathleen Harrigan for her constant support and inspiration,*

*and to Kathleen Donaughy, Lorraine Mihill, Mike Edwards, Evelyn Cook and Danny Koelle for their excellent advice, suggestions and enthusiasm.*

Made in the USA
Las Vegas, NV
29 December 2020

14828503R00135